MW01126490

COTTON

Satan's Fury MC

L. Wilder

Cotton
Satan's Fury MC
Copyright © 2016 L. Wilder
Print Edition

All rights reserved. Without limiting the rights under copyright reserved above, no part of this publication or any part of this series may be reproduced without the prior written permission of both the copyright owner and the above publisher of this book.

This book is a work of fiction. Some of the places named in the book are actual places found in Paris, TN. The names, characters, brands, and incidents are either the product of the author's imagination or are used fictitiously. The author acknowledges the trademarked status and owners of various products and locations referenced in this work of fiction, which have been used without permission. The publication or use of these trademarks is not authorized, associated with, or sponsored by the trademark owners.

Warning: This book is intended for readers 18 years or older due to bad language, violence, and explicit sex scenes.

Cover Model – Joseph Cannata:
www.facebook.com/joseph.cannata

Cover Design – LJ Anderson:
www.facebook.com/lj.anderson.33

Editor – Julia Goda:
www.facebook.com/juliagodaeditingservices

Marci Ponce – Content Editing

Book Teasers and Design – Monica Langley Holloway:
www.facebook.com/Kustombooks2reviews

Dedication

To My Dad

For always being there when I need you.

Prologue

MY FATHER ALWAYS said it took a strong man to admit his mistakes, and an even stronger man to learn from those mistakes. The crazy thing was I never saw him make a mistake. Everyone looked up to my father, especially me. He was the kind of man who thought a handshake was enough; and where he was concerned, it was. He never broke his word, even when it was difficult to follow through. He never failed to provide for his family, giving us a life where we all felt safe and loved. He adored my mother with a passion that never seemed to waiver, making us all love him even more. I wanted to be just like him, but it just wasn't in the cards for me.

Born towheaded and full of mischief, I was the oldest of three sons. My dad got a kick out of my snow-white hair and nicknamed me Cotton, saying that one day I'd prosper just like the cotton fields in Tennessee. Even when my hair turned dark brown like his own, the nickname stuck. There was no doubt I held a special place in my father's heart; we could all see it. His eyes gleamed with pride whenever I was around. I knew he had high expectations for me, wanting me to be a good role model for my brothers, Joseph and Lucas; but more times than not, I found myself in some kind of trouble I had no business getting into. I just couldn't stop myself. It was nothing for us to sneak off in the middle of the day when we were supposed to be helping out at the house; or in the middle of the night when we should've been sleeping soundly. There was nothing better than running amuck with my brothers; and with them falling close behind, I sought to discover all the secrets the world had hidden within her. There wasn't a tree tall enough or a cave dark enough to deter my curiosity. While Joe and Luke would stand by watching, I'd slip into the dark depths of a cave, unaffected by the voice inside my head that screamed for me to turn back. I got a rush from the danger that lurked inside, drawing me in, deeper and deeper into the darkness. Maybe it had something to do with being the first-born son, or maybe it was just a part of who I was, but nothing could stop that restless feeling I felt stirring in my gut. More times than not, my brothers and I found ourselves in a heap of trouble, and there was nothing worse than seeing that look of disappointment in my father's eyes when we screwed up. Unfortunately, it happened a lot; but it didn't prevent us from doing it time and time again, knowing our father would always be there to help pull us out of trouble... until the day he wasn't.

When my father died, a part of me died with him, and the direction of my life changed forever. As I grew older, I always tried to remember what he said about being a strong man... a good man. In the life I've lived, I have made my mistakes—lots of them—but I've never had a problem admitting when I fucked up. The hard part wasn't learning from the mistakes I'd made; it was finding a way to fix them.

Chapter 1

COTTON

Sophomore Year of High School

I WAS FOURTEEN when my father shocked us all by dying of a massive heart attack. His death damn near destroyed our family, ending the safe and secure world I'd always known. My mother hadn't worked in years, making it difficult for her to find a job that could sustain the life we'd grown accustomed to. When she'd finally managed to find a few odd jobs, it just wasn't enough, and I was overcome with the need to protect my mother and brothers. I loved them and couldn't stand to see the worry in their eyes. I knew I had to do something, anything to make things better for them. I started mowing lawns and running the local paper route, helping out the only way I knew how. I was doing all I could, and we were still barely able to pay our bills. That's when my Uncle Saul stepped in, helping out in a way I couldn't.

Until then, I really didn't know much about my uncle, other than he was the president of some motorcycle club. I didn't know why we never spent time with him or his family, but I'd gotten the impression a long time ago that it had something to do with my mother. A look of disgust would cross her face whenever my dad mentioned his brother's name or his club, and eventually, he just stopped talking about him altogether. It was obvious to all of us she didn't care for him or what he represented, but at the time, she was in no position to turn down his offer to help. I never did understand her distaste for him. I liked Saul from the start. I could see my father when I looked into his eyes or heard his voice, reminding me of that secure feeling I had whenever my dad was around. I felt a pull to my uncle, and each time he'd come by the house, I'd stare out the window and watch as he pulled up on his motorcycle. There was a mystery to him that intrigued me, making me want to know more about his life and his club that existed on the outside of town.

Years passed, and even though I knew my mother wouldn't approve, I asked my uncle if he could help me find a more substantial job, thinking the money would help out with the bills. I'd heard him talking about a house renovation the club was doing for one of their members, and since I was good with my hands, I hoped he'd be able to find a place for me. When I brought it up to Uncle Saul, I figured he would say no because of my age, but I knew I had my father's build which made me look older than I really was, so I took a chance. At first he hesitated, but after I explained it would really help us out and promised to keep up my grades up at school, he finally agreed. It didn't take me long to realize the job I so desperately wanted wasn't exactly what I thought it would be. Since I was much younger than any of the club members, they had me doing all the grunt work that they didn't want to do themselves. I'd never worked harder in my life, but I liked being there, working with all of those men my uncle called his brothers, and soon began to feel like I was a part of something more than just a work crew. I felt like I belonged, especially when they'd let me tag along on some of their rides to blow off steam after work. Being on a bike with them was all that I thought it would be and more. The only thing better would have been having one of my own.

I'd been working with them for almost six months—we had finished one brother's house and had moved on to the next—when my cousin, Derek, showed up on the work site, and as soon as he stepped out of his truck, it was clear to us all he was on a war path. At first glance, he reminded me a lot of Uncle Saul with his tall, thick build and coal-black hair, but unlike his father, his greenish-blue eyes showed no warmth behind them. I watched as he stormed over to Doc with his fists clenched and a scowl on his face, all the while grumbling curses under his breath. Doc wasn't the kind of man who took shit from anyone, especially some angry kid. He was a retired military medic, and he expected respect, and he always received from his crew. After a brief one-sided argument, Derek's face flashed red with anger. While grumbling under his breath, he grabbed one of the tool belts off of the table and walked over to me. He gave me a quick grunt and chin lift, then immediately got to work. It was almost an hour later before he ever actually spoke to me.

"You actually *wanted* to work here with these fuckers?" he asked with a frustrated look.

"Yeah. Guess I did," I confessed.

"You got a screw loose or something?" he huffed. He didn't wait for me to answer before he said, "Pop's all pissed 'cause I got pulled over for speeding last night. It wouldn't have been a big deal if that nosy ass cop hadn't gone digging in the back of my truck and found the cooler of beer and my bag of pot. He blew a gasket when he had to bail me out of jail again. Told me I had to work out here as my fucking punishment, but the old man's got another thing coming if he thinks I'm going do this shit for free," he complained.

"That's a tough break," I responded, not really knowing what to say.

"Ah, hell. This isn't the first time, and it won't be the last," he laughed. I looked over at him, noticing the mischievous smirk that spread across his face. There was something about that look that set me on edge, but I quickly forgot about it when he said, "You should come out with me and the guys tomorrow night. Some of us are heading over to Mindy's party after the football game."

I was only a sophomore at the time and spent most of my time working or helping my mother out with my brothers, so I hadn't gone to many high school parties. I couldn't help but get a little excited about going to one of Mindy's blowouts. Trying not to sound too eager, I said, "Yeah, that'd be cool. I'll just meet you at the game."

I spent the next few hours listening to Derek gripe and groan as we finished the last of the demolition. By the time I finally made it home, I was beyond exhausted, and it was all I could do to take a shower before I crashed for the night. The next day, everybody was hyped up about the party. It was all anyone was talking about, and by the time we pulled up at Mindy's house, the place was packed. The music was blaring through the house as I followed Derek and his buddies through the crowd and into the kitchen. We shuffled through the different groups of popular kids, each one totally absorbed in their own conversation, until we passed a couple of seniors. They glared at Derek as he passed by them, making it known to everyone they weren't happy about him being there, but Derek didn't care. He didn't give a shit what anyone thought of him, and it showed. He had an air of confidence that was almost too much for me to bear, but his friends ate it up, laughing and carrying on right along with him. They were like a pack of wild dogs sniffing through the crowd, marking their territory along the way, and I found myself wishing I'd skipped the party altogether.

We'd been there for almost an hour when Derek came over to me and asked, "You ready for another one?"

I was on my fourth beer and already feeling a buzz when he handed me another full cup. With a wicked grin, he pulled out several pills from his back pocket and dropped them into his drink. After swirling it around for a few seconds, he said, "I'll be right back."

I was surprised to see that he was heading over to Sara Locke, one of the girls from the club. Her father was one of the brothers of Satan's Fury, but that didn't seem to slow him down. In fact, from the way he was eye fucking her, he obviously had a thing for her. Sara was a little younger than most of the girls at the party, but she was by far the most attractive around.

She was wearing a short skirt with black cowboy boots and a sweater with a slight V, showing off all of her curves. Her long, dark hair fell loose around her shoulders and barely covered her breasts. There was no doubt about it—she was a fucking knockout. When Sara noticed Derek walking in her direction, she glared at him suspiciously, her fierce, blue eyes watching his every move. A lustful smile spread across Derek's face as he approached her and offered her his drink. She hesitantly took the drink from his hand and seemed leery as she studied what was inside the cup. For several seconds, she just held the cup in her hand, swishing it from side to side, but when her friend encouraged her to take a drink, all of her doubts were quickly forgotten. Just as she brought the cup to her mouth, Derek glanced back at me and winked, giving me an evil grin. He continued to talk to Sara and her friends for a few more minutes, then he playfully swatted her on the ass before strutting back over to me.

"What the fuck did you just do?" I barked.

"Relax, man. I just got the party started, brother," he snickered. "Nothing better than easy pussy."

"You fucking drugged her?" I roared.

"Fuck, yeah, I did. Now keep your damn voice down."

"Look, man, I've got no problem if the chick is willing, and hell, Sara looks hot tonight...

damn hot. I'd be all over that shit, but taking what hasn't been offered isn't an option."

"Didn't realize you were such a fucking tight ass, Cotton. Guess I was wrong about you after all," he huffed, then turned back to his buddies, bragging once again about what he'd just done.

Everyone except Derek's crew seemed completely unaware of what had taken place, which pissed me off even more. I couldn't take my eyes off Sara, but I wasn't the only one. Derek was watching her like a hawk, waiting for his drugs to kick in. Seeing the hungry look in his eyes when he ogled her repulsed me even more. The guy had no honor, no reservations about what he was doing, and I hated him for it. I had no idea how many girls had come before Sara, but I refused to let him get away with it again. Along with one of Derek's sidekicks, I noticed that her eyes were glassing over and her balance was off, but I caught my break when several girls approached Derek and his buddies. They were momentarily distracted and didn't see Sara when she started staggering toward the stairs. Knowing it might be my only chance to help her, I cautiously followed and found her in Mindy's parents' room. I'd prayed Derek had just been fucking around, but when I found Sara's lifeless body sprawled out across the bed, there was no doubt he'd drugged her. She was completely out of it, and I knew I had to do whatever I could to protect her.

When I heard Derek's voice drawing closer, I rushed over and locked the door. I turned back, glancing at Sara lying there on the bed, and it was all I could do to keep from slamming my fist through the wall. I wanted to stomp Derek's ass, but unfortunately, I knew I couldn't take him on with all of his buddies in tow. There were just too many of them and they weren't the type to fight fair. When I heard the taunting shouts of my name vibrating through the walls, I knew I had to act fast. Trying to buy myself some time, I grabbed a chair and propped it against the door, bracing it firmly, so no one could get in.

The doorknob turned and jolted, and when it didn't open, Derek started pounding on the door. "Cotton, I know your ass is in there. Open the fucking door."

"Not going to happen, *Derek*. Just back the hell off," I roared.

"You've got thirty seconds to open this god-damn door, or I am going to knock the motherfucker down," he barked.

"Yeah… you go ahead and do that. Won't take any time for everyone to come running to see what's going on up here. Either way, this thing with you and Sara isn't gonna happen," I scoffed.

"The hell it isn't! She's mine, motherfucker, and there's nothing you can do to stop me from having her!" he shouted as his fist slammed into

the door once again. "Open the fucking door!...
Fuck! You're dead, Cotton! Dead!"

Knowing I was running out of time, I picked
up the house phone and dialed 911. When I
heard the operator answer, I laid the receiver on
the bed next to Sara, rushed over to the window,
and slipped out onto the roof.

As soon as my feet hit the ground, I heard
someone shout, *"There he is! Hey, Derek. He's out
back."*

I knew things were about to go south, so I
took off running, hoping like hell I might have a
chance to make it to the railroad tracks before
they could catch me. I was wrong, and it cost me.
I'd barely made it a half a mile down the road
when Derek's truck pulled up next to me, and
one of the guys jumped out and tackled me to
the ground. Even though he was much bigger
than me, I managed to get back on my feet, but
in a matter of seconds, all six of them were on
top of me. I did my best to fight them off, but it
was difficult with all of them coming at me at
once. I was holding my own until Derek
slammed some kind of board across my chest,
cracking several of my ribs with the force of the
hit. When he hit me with it again, the pain got to
be too much, and I dropped to my knees, unable
to defend myself any longer. After that, everything was just a blur. Their grunts echoed around
me as they plowed their feet into my side, chest,

back, and head over and over again. I was just about to pass out when I heard police sirens coming down the road toward Mindy's house.

"Fuck! Get in the damn truck," Derek barked.

"You're just gonna leave him here?" one of them asked. "Shouldn't we take him off somewhere so nobody can find him?"

"We don't have time. Get your ass in the truck," he ordered.

I'm not sure how long I lay out there in the dark before Doc found me. I barely remember anything after Derek's truck drove off down the road, leaving me there to die. I woke up the next day in a room I'd never seen before, feeling like I had been put through a fucking meat grinder. Doc was standing over in the corner, talking to Uncle Saul, and I could see the concern in their eyes as they spoke.

When Uncle Saul looked over to me and saw I was awake, he walked over to the bed and rested his hand on my shoulder as he said, "You're gonna be okay, Cotton. Doc found you lying on the side of the road on his way in this morning. He almost passed you by, thinking you were some drunk, but when he saw that Mariner's baseball jacket of yours, he realized it was you. He was just going to take you on home until he saw the condition you were in."

I tried to sit up on the bed, but stopped when a pain shot through my side. Fuck. They'd done quite a number on me. My left eye was almost swollen shut, and my entire body was covered with bruises. I started to feel a little dizzy, so I laid my head back down on the pillow. Knowing I would've been in even worse shape if it weren't for Doc, I turned to him and said, "Thanks, Doc. Appreciate you helping me out."

"No problem, kid. You took one hell of a beating last night. Glad I came across you when I did."

As soon as he left the room, Uncle Saul said, "Just so we're clear. I know what happened last night. All of it. Sara's still a little out of sorts, but she'll be fine. Luckily, her father is a brother of the club, so the situation has been dealt with. And Derek... he will be dealt with as soon as I leave here. You can count on that." He took a deep breath, then continued, "You did good helping Sara last night. Glad you were there. She's family, and we do what we can to protect what's ours. You're already showing you can be trusted to do just that. Now, get some rest. I'll be back to check on you in a few hours."

Just before he walked out the door, I called out to him. "Uncle Saul... what about my mom? She was expecting me home last night and she's ..."

"Don't worry about her. Just get some rest and plan on staying here at the club for the rest of the weekend. I'll come up with something to tell your mother," he assured me.

I spent the next few days mending and learning my way around the clubhouse. I often worried about what was going on at home, but Uncle Saul assured me that my mom and brothers were fine. He'd told her I was helping one of the brother's out with a side job, and he'd make sure I got to school on Monday. I had no idea how he got her to go along with it—I was just glad he did. While I was there, I decided to make the best of it. I'd always wanted to know what it was like at the club, and since I was going to be staying for several days, I finally had my chance to see it for myself. Being there was everything I thought it would be and more. The clubhouse wasn't just a place to meet and drink beer, or even a place to work—it was home. The guys treated me like I was one of their own, and I found myself wanting to stay... even if I had to deal with Derek. I kept expecting to run into him, but he never showed. Later, I found out Uncle Saul had been true to his word, and Derek had been punished. After one hell of a beating from Sara's dad, Uncle Saul cut him off, telling him he wouldn't get another dime from him until he cleaned up his act. That never happened.

Instead, he'd stolen money from a notorious drug dealer on the east side of town, and the trouble with Derek only escalated from there. He was set on a path no one could deter him from, and in the end, it cost him everything.

Chapter 2

CASSIDY

Present Day

"SO, IT'S OFFICIAL," Henley laughed. "You're an old lady."

"Never thought I'd be happy to be called that," Wren laughed. I smiled at her, trying to hide the loneliness I'd been feeling since the lockdown had started. Cotton and I hadn't been together long. We'd barely even started to explore whatever was going on with us, but since the lockdown, he hadn't even talked to me—much less touched me. It was hard to swallow my jealousy when I thought about Wren and Stitch. There was a time when I thought Stitch would never take on an old lady. He was the club Enforcer, and his mind was always focused on his brothers. But even with everything that was going on with the club, he'd managed to fall head over heels in love with Wren and her son, Wyatt. It'd just been a few months, but they were already making plans on becoming a family. I hated myself for feeling anything but happy for them both, but it was hard. I wanted that with Cotton, but he'd never taken that step, and since the lockdown, it didn't look like he ever would.

Emerson, Stitch's sister, leaned forward and grinned as she teased Wren, "Are you sure you're up for this? Griffin can be pretty bossy."

"I think I can handle it," she blushed.

"I never thought I'd see him so happy. I'm so glad he found you," Emerson continued.

"I think this calls for a celebration," I announced, trying my best to put on a smile. "Who's up for a round of shots?"

"Ah… you and the damn shots. Are you trying to kill me?" Henley whined. "It's been days, and I still haven't gotten over it."

Remembering how sick she'd gotten, I rolled my eyes and teased, "Well, nobody shoved them down your throat, sis."

"Well, I totally blame you for the worst hangover in the world! I don't know if I'll ever be able to drink again! Just looking at those limes makes me want to gag! You're supposed to watch out for your *little* sister," Henley feigned a pout.

"Yeah, well, that's a full-time job, kiddo," I laughed. So much had changed with Henley over the last six months. I'd been bartending at the club for over a year and only managed to convince her to come hang out with me a couple of times while I worked. She usually had an excuse for staying behind, saying she had to cram for a test or work on one of her school projects. But after she witnessed the brutal murder of Skidrow, Satan's Fury's Sergeant of Arms, she no longer had a choice. The brothers of the club were determined to protect her, and whether she liked it or not, they'd do whatever it took to keep her safe. As fate would have it, Maverick was put in charge of keeping an eye on her. Henley didn't make it easy on him, and there were times when I almost felt sorry for the guy. But despite their rocky beginning, Maverick found something special in Henley, quickly claiming her as his own and risking everything to protect her. I had no doubt she'd met her match with Maverick, and I was happy for her, glad that she'd found some-one who would always put her life before his own. They were always together, which meant she was at the club all the time. I've enjoyed having her around, but since the mandatory lockdown, she'd been moody and a bit of a handful.

"I'll have one," Allie answered with a smile as she looked behind her, checking to see if her husband was still playing pool. "Maybe two if Guardrail's game doesn't end soon."

I reached behind the bar for the large bottle of tequila and placed it on the counter next to the salt and limes I'd put out earlier. I filled each

of the shot glasses, and we each took our turn
tilting our heads back, downing our drinks, and
wincing as the burn of the alcohol hit the backs
of our throats. We'd been talking for almost an
hour, and I was just about to pour everyone
another round of drinks, when Cotton came in
and sat down at the end of the bar. Tension
washed over me as I quickly glanced over at him,
all the while pretending I hadn't even seen him
walk in.

When I let out a deep sigh, Wren asked, "Are
you okay?"

I smiled and said, "I'm fine. I just need
to …"

"Cass," Cotton interrupted me as he called
out to me from the other end of the bar.

"Well, shit," I grumbled under my breath.
Since he hadn't spoken to me in days, it was hard
to even look at him. It wasn't that he hadn't been
around. In fact, he was around all the damn time,
watching my every move like a hawk. I knew the
issues with the club were getting to him and I
hated to see him on edge, but I didn't like the
silent treatment he'd been dishing out over the
last few weeks. I tried to blow it off, but I missed
him, plain and simple. I didn't want him to know
that his new found distance was getting to me,
but I couldn't help myself. Every time he was
around, I lost my sense of reason. I had to stop
letting him get to me so much. He might be the

President of Satan's Fury MC, protector and leader of the club and everyone involved in it, but that didn't mean he could control how I felt. It was up to me to get a grip and stop letting the man get to me so much. Feigning indifference, I flicked my hair over my shoulder and looked over to him as I said, "Yeah?"

"Need a beer," he ordered, barely even looking in my damn direction. Asshole.

"And?" I asked, placing my hand on my hip. I wanted to be mad at him, wanted to hate him for making me feel the way I did about him, but just seeing him sitting there, looking sexy as hell, was making me lose all of my resolve.

His eyebrows furrowed in annoyance as he repeated, "*Cass*."

I let out a deep breath, and since I knew it was pointless to resist him, I finally gave in. With my eyes locked on his, I walked over to him at the end of the bar. I reached into the cooler to get his beer, and without wiping the water that dripped from the bottle, I sat it on the counter in front of him. His eyes dropped to the water that pooled around the bottle as he let out a disgruntled sigh.

"You got something you want to say?" he asked with a low, raspy voice.

I took in a deep breath, letting the scent of his cologne surround me as I tried to think of something clever to say, but it was no use. I hadn't talked to him in days and being so close to him had my brain turning to mush. It didn't help that under his cut he was wearing my favorite gray t-shirt that showed off the definition of his perfect damn chest, and those faded jeans that made me want to reach out and grab his ass. Shit. My eyes dropped to his perfect, full lips, and I couldn't stop myself from remembering all the wicked things that he could do with his mouth. Just thinking about kissing him made me want to run my fingers through his salt and pepper hair. Damn. It was too much. I needed to touch him, to feel his body pressed against mine again, and act on all those crazy feelings I'd been having for him. I wanted to tell him how much he meant to me, but I couldn't cross that imaginary line we'd drawn so many months ago. He'd kept things simple, never letting me know for certain that he felt the same way about me. But I wasn't blind. I could see the way he looked at me, the longing behind those beautiful, dark eyes. But he'd never said the words. He'd never made any declaration of how he felt about me whatsofreakingever. I wasn't the kind of girl who threw herself at any man, no matter how desperately I might want him. Nothing real was going to happen with us until he took that first step.

With all the sarcasm I could muster, I said, "*Nope*. All good here."

When he sat there, silently staring at me, I

turned my back to him and started to leave, only to stop dead in my tracks when his fingers wrapped around my elbow, pulling me over to him. When I looked up at him and noticed the intense expression on his face, I froze. I could only stand there silently staring at him.

"I think you have something to say," he pushed. He was right. I did have something to say... hell, I had plenty to say, but I couldn't. Maybe I was too proud. Maybe I was just a coward, but I just couldn't take the chance. When I didn't answer him, he stood up, towering over me with a disapproving look.

"What exactly do you want from me, Cotton?" I snapped. "What is it that you want me to say?" I could've said a thousand things, but as usual, I said the wrong damn thing at the wrong damn time. He quickly stood up and walked over to me. Without saying a word, he took my hand and pulled me down the hall. When we got to his room, he opened the door and led me inside. After he finally released me, I was left standing in the middle of the room while he stood several feet away from me with his arms crossed and a curious look on his face. The silence was deafening as we stood there, staring at one another, and when I couldn't take it any longer, I cocked my head to the side and asked, "You got something you want to say?"

I watched with apprehension as he took a

step toward me, staring at me like a predator studying its prey. My heart started pounding against my chest, and without me even realizing it, I began backing away from him, only stopping when my back hit the wall. In just a blink, he was there, hovering over me in all his glory, and seeing the look of lust in his eyes made all of my angst about his feelings quickly fade away.

"I can't do this anymore," he said softly.

"Can't do what?" When he didn't answer, I asked again. "What can't you do anymore, Cotton?" At that moment, it was if I was watching all of his walls fall down right there in front of me, leaving me with a Cotton I almost didn't recognize. He looked so vulnerable standing there, making me want to wrap my arms around him.

"This thing between you and me. Cass, you know… you've always known," he whispered, the warmth of his breath caressing my cheek. I could see the longing in his eyes, and I couldn't imagine wanting him any more than I did at that moment, but it just wasn't enough.

"I've waited, Cotton… all this time, but all I've gotten is silence from you. So, now I need the words. I need you to tell me," I pushed, but he said nothing, not with words, yet the burning in his eyes continued to lure me in.

"Cotton?"

Still no answer. Instead, his hand slipped behind me, pulling me closer to him, and when he looked down at me with those dark, piercing eyes, my world stopped turning. The only thing left between us was the anticipation of our lips meeting once again, filling the air around us with want and need. When he finally lowered his mouth to mine, the anticipation didn't end, it was just the beginning. His tongue brushed against mine, and I felt an electric shock shoot up my spine, setting off an explosion of desire that couldn't be contained. It was all I could do not to completely unravel in his arms.

He released my mouth just long enough to say, "I've tried to stay away… thought it was the best way to protect you. I thought I wasn't good for you. I wanted you to have only the best, but I can't do it anymore. I'm just too selfish."

It was finally happening, the moment I'd been thinking about… dreaming about for all these months, and I wanted to remember every detail—the scent of his skin, the warmth of his touch, the taste of his mouth. My hands wound around his neck, and my fingers raked through his thick, dark hair as he deepened the kiss. I knew then that everything had changed. We both knew it. In true Cotton form, he had given me my answer—and what an answer it was.

Chapter 3

COTTON

FOR ME, BEING with Cassidy was like that kick you get out of that first cup of coffee in the morning. I was always surprised by the charge I got whenever she walked into the room—a feeling that hit me deep down in my gut. I couldn't get enough. Nothing had ever made me feel that way, not since I was a kid on Christmas morning. There was something about her that captivated me, like she knew something nobody else knew—some great secret you just wish to hell you could figure out. She was beautiful, so damn beautiful, but it was so much more than that. It was the way her smile would light up a room, the sexy sway of her hips when she danced, and even the way she tucked her hair behind her ear when she was nervous about something. It was the way she'd sing to herself as she worked behind the bar, completely unaware that the minute she opened her mouth, she'd cast a spell on everyone around her, captivating us all with the magic of her voice—especially me. She was strong and determined, but there was a soft side to her, almost fragile. The brothers respected her, knowing she'd do anything to make sure they had whatever they needed. It amazed me. In such a short time, she'd become invaluable to us all, always putting the needs of the club first.

There was so much about her I was drawn to, but it was her spark that got to me the most. I couldn't end my day without getting that kick I got whenever I saw her, making me feel like the world wasn't so bad after all. It gave me strength. It gave me hope. I knew my brothers thought I was trying to keep her for myself, but that wasn't it. I couldn't take the chance that one of them might hurt her... destroy her light. I had to protect her, even if that meant protecting her from me. I just couldn't take it if something happened to that spark, and I was determined to make sure it stayed just the way it was. I'd done what I could to keep my distance, thinking I was protecting her, but I was done with that.

She stood there, looking like every man's wet dream with the curls of her long, brown hair flowing loose around her shoulders. Her short skirt inched up her thigh, showing off her long, lean legs, and her dark blue sweater showed off her perfect curves, making me want her more than my next breath. Without warning, without permission… without thinking about the consequences, I lowered my mouth to hers, kissing her with heat, and angst, and promise of what was to come. The beat of her heart next to mine calmed me, refueled me, and that's when I knew. She wasn't my first, but she would be my *last*. I pulled her closer as I continued to devour her mouth, claiming her in the only way I could in that moment. Damn. I loved how her body instantly responded to mine, but it made it damn near impossible to not take her over to my bed and finish what I'd started. I reluctantly pulled back and asked, "You still need the words?"

When she nodded, I continued, "The day you walked into my club, I knew there was something about you I had to have, but nothing could have prepared me for the first time I had you in my bed. After that, I was done. I can't get you out of my head. You're in my every thought. I can't even escape you in my dreams. You keep drawing me in, and I am helpless to stop it."

With her face flushed red, she answered, "I think I got it." A small grin slowly spread across her face as she tucked a loose strand of her hair behind her ear, letting me know I was getting to her.

I brought my hands up to her face, gently brushing my thumb across her cheek as I said, "You're the favorite part of my day, Cass. Just one look at you, and the rest of the world just fades away."

Her eyebrows furrowed when she asked, "I've waited so long for you to say something. I hoped there was something more between us, but I was beginning to think it was all in my head. But I've gotta ask... Why now? After all this time, why did you choose tonight to tell me all this?"

She knew me too well. After fending off a major attack on our club's territory, only to find out that my cousin, Derek, was behind it all, I realized life is just too damn short. I'd fucked up by keeping my distance, but I couldn't leave this world without telling her how I felt. I knew it was selfish of me, especially since I had no idea how things with Derek were going to turn out, but in the end, I was just a man—a man completely captivated by the woman who stood in front of him, and I couldn't wait a moment longer to have her.

"You needed the words," I teased, hoping she wouldn't push for an answer I couldn't give. Before she had a chance to question me further, there was a thundering knock at my door.

"Cotton?" Big Mike called out.

"Yeah?"

"You got a minute?" he asked. "Something's come up. It's important."

Cass gave me a nod, letting me know she understood club business came first. Turning my head toward the door, I shouted, "Need a minute. Office in five."

"Sure thing, Prez."

I waited until I heard him head down the hall, then I turned back to Cass and said, "We're not done here. Not by a long shot."

A sexy grin spread across her face as she said, "Good to know. I'll be here when you get done. For now, I need to get back out to the bar and see to my girls." She lifted herself up on her tiptoes and kissed me, making my dick strain against my zipper as she took her time exploring every inch of my mouth. When she was done, she looked up at me and winked before heading toward the door. Just before she walked out of the room, she looked back over to me and said, "Just so you know… you are the best part of my day, too."

I followed Cass out of the room and headed straight to my office. His timing couldn't have been worse, but I was eager to see what had come up with Big Mike. Our club was under attack, had been for weeks, and when we discovered Derek's face on the surveillance video, I knew things were only going to get worse. Derek wasn't only after our territory. He was after revenge, plain and simple, and I was going to do everything in my power to make sure he didn't get it. But before I could stop him, I had to find him. That's where Big Mike came into play. If anyone could find that piece of shit, it was Big Mike. When I reached my office door, he was standing there, waiting for me. He had several folders in his hand, and I could tell from the look on his face that he was anxious.

"Whatcha got?"

"Right now, I've got more questions than I do answers. I need some help filling in the blanks."

I opened the door to my office and motioned for him to follow me inside. As I sat down at my desk, I said, "What do you need from me?"

"Your history with the club... how it all started and how it all led to Derek losing his shit," he replied.

"Hell, that was a lifetime ago. I wouldn't even know where to start." Big Mike wasn't the kind of guy who skimped on details, so I wasn't surprised he had questions about our past. Actually, it's one of the reasons he's the best.

He took the seat in front of my desk and said, "Just start at the beginning. I want to know anything and everything you can remember. It doesn't matter how insignificant. There has to be something that might help me put the pieces together."

Needing a smoke, I reached in my pocket and grabbed my pack of cigarettes. I quickly lit one and took a long drag before I said, "As you know, I got my in with the club when I started working for Uncle Saul. I didn't officially start prospecting until the summer after my junior year of high school and didn't patch in until I was almost nineteen, right after I graduated. By then, both my brothers had started prospecting." I took another pull from my cigarette as I thought about everything Uncle Saul had done for my family. He was a guiding force in our lives, and I missed having him around. I exhaled, then continued, "We were young. Hell, we were the youngest to ever join the club, but we all knew this was the only life for us. We just had to graduate first. Uncle Saul wouldn't have it any other way. We were family, and he was like a father to all of us."

"And Derek?" Mike pushed.

"Derek was just a piece of shit. Always has been, always will be. I tried to make the best of it with him, but just never really trusted the guy. Hell, none of us did. He couldn't stand the fact his father had chosen to take me under his wing, teaching me everything I needed to know about running the club." I took another drag of my cigarette, then after I exhaled slowly, I continued, "Uncle Saul had only been working with me a few years when he had the accident. It was tough, but he gave it a good fight. When he didn't fully recover, he gave me the nod to take the gavel, and with the club's unanimous agreement, I was voted in as President."

"Did you ever wonder if Derek had anything to do with your uncle's motorcycle accident?"

"Yeah, but none of us were ever able to tie it to him. I knew in my gut he was behind it and wanted to make him pay for what he'd done, but it was Uncle Saul's last order as President for us to let it ride."

Mike looked down at the folders in his hands and started rifling through them. When he found what he was looking for, he asked, "What about his mom? Were they close?"

"I wouldn't call them close, but it wasn't because of Aunt Gracie. Hell, she was always trying, but Derek wasn't having any part of it.

"I think I found something. It might be the link we've been missing. Your aunt had a sister named Gertie who lived in Alberta." He stopped just long enough to show me a picture of a woman who looked a lot like my aunt, then he continued, "She rented out her upstairs apartment to a man named Logan Stewart around the time when Derek left Clallam County. He was about the same age as Derek, and there is no record of him before he moved into Gertie's apartment. Now, here's where things get interesting." He handed me another picture of Gertie, standing next to a man wearing a biker's cut, and said, "Her husband was a member of a small MC that had connections with several clubs in Alaska... including Anchorage."

"Okay. So talk me through all of this. Are you thinking Derek is this Logan Stewart? And if so, how does that help us find him now?"

"All it takes is one connection. We work off this Logan Stewart intel, and find one person who Derek is associated with now. Then, it's just a matter of tracing their steps. One swipe of a credit card, and we have him." It sounded simple enough, but I knew nothing with Derek had ever been simple.

"I want this done, Big," I grumbled. "Don't care what it takes."

He stood to leave, but before he walked out of my office, he turned to me and said, "We'll get 'em, Prez. We're close. I can feel it."

As soon as he was gone, I reached into my desk and pulled out the folder he'd given us a few weeks ago. Big had been able to pull all the intel off of one of Derek's computers, which gave us all the information he'd been able to uncover about every brother in the club. Each folder contained all the intimate details of our lives, including pictures Derek had taken over the past six months, pictures of us and the people we cared about. I sifted through all the pictures of Cass. Damn. She was beautiful. My stomach turned at the thought of him even looking at her, much less watching her every move. The pictures were very detailed, letting me know she'd sparked an interest in Derek, and it pissed me the hell off.

I knew how obsessed he could become over something he wanted. I continued to flip through the pictures until I came across a couple of old shots of Sara and I together. I had no idea where Derek had managed to find them. I hadn't seen any of them in years. We were at the clubhouse, celebrating Sara's high school graduation. We'd been dating for almost a year, and back then, we were crazy about each other. I studied the photo, first noticing the bright smile on Sara's face and then my own. We were happy. I remembered how we talked about plans to conquer the world together, but life got in the way. I glanced back down at the picture, and that's when I noticed Derek lurking in the back corner of the clubhouse bar, gawking at Sara. I wasn't surprised. We all knew Derek was obsessed with her. Hell, he'd almost gotten himself killed when he tried to drug and rape her, but even that didn't stop him from pursuing her. He was always pushing her to go out with him, and even tried to convince her I'd been unfaithful a couple of times. She never listened and just continued to ignore him, which only made him angrier with me. Luckily, Derek's lust over Sara settled down when she left for college. His interests were quickly drawn elsewhere, and he'd soon forgotten about Sara… or so I'd thought.

I spent the next hour going through everything Mike had uncovered about Logan Stewart and eventually made a connection. I was able to lock in on two possible aliases Derek had used since he left and found two clubs he'd had dealings with over the past year. We were finally making headway, and it was only a matter of time before we found him. Derek's little game of cat and mouse was coming to an end.

Chapter 4

CASSIDY

H ENLEY WAS SITTING at the bar with her hand resting under her chin, looking like she hadn't slept in days. I sat a bottle of water in front of her and asked, "Are you going to tell me why you have those dark circles under your eyes?"

"I don't know. I'm just tired, I guess. I'd do just about anything to sleep in my own bed tonight," she pouted. "I mean… I've enjoyed being at the club and all, but this lockdown is getting old. I miss my big, fluffy pillows and my soft down comforter. Maverick's stupid mattress is hard as a rock."

Laughing, I said, "Well, tell him it's time to get a new one."

"It is a new one! Apparently, he didn't get the memo that beds are actually supposed to be comfortable." She took a sip of her water, then said, "Don't mind me. I'll get over it."

"Maybe you're coming down with something. You don't look so good, sis."

"Yeah, it's probably just a bug or something. I'll feel better in a couple of days," she assured me.

"If you aren't feeling better by tomorrow, you should let Doc check you out."

"Okay. Enough about me. You gonna tell me what the *Old Man* had to say?" Henley smirked. I rolled my eyes at her, and when I didn't immediately answer her, she kept at it. "You know, you took the whole *old man* thing to another level," she laughed.

"Stop it, Henley. Cotton is not *old*!"

She leaned forward and with a mischievous grin, she whispered, "Don't get me wrong. The man is hot… and since he shaved that god awful goatee, he's smokin'… but yeah… he's still old."

"He's only forty-four years old. That's not old!" I knew she was just trying to mess with my head, but I couldn't help but feel defensive. I was crazy about him, and since she was my sister, a part of me needed her approval. "And I kinda liked the goatee."

"No, you didn't! He looks way better without it. Besides, now I'm not so tempted to call him *sir*," she laughed. Feeling frustrated, I grabbed a towel and started cleaning the counter. My mind instantly went to Cotton, remembering some of the moments we'd shared together over the past year, and I realized I never really thought of Cotton as old—far from it. I'd seen glimpses of another side to him—a fun, youthful side— where he was truly happy, and I actually got to see him smiling. I can still remember the deep rumble of his laughter when he took me out on an unexpected day of exploring. It was one of the last warm days before winter, and we were just supposed to go for a quick run for the club, but his little detour took me on an adventure I'll never forget.

"Got something I want to show you," he announced as he turned down a gravel road. His SUV jolted from side-to-side when it hit one of the many potholes along the old road, but Cotton never let off the accelerator. I had no idea where he was taking me, but he was obviously eager to get there. When the truck started climbing up the mountain, making the engine hum as it resisted the steep incline, curiosity started to get the best of me.

"Where exactly are we going?" I asked.

"A special place," he announced, and when he smiled, I could see the kid in him, carefree and ready for anything. "It's somewhere I used to go with my brothers when we were kids."

When I was hit with the familiar scent of the ocean, I realized we were headed to Cape Flattery. I'd been there many times with my family, but we'd never taken the route Cotton was taking. It was filled with sharp turns, and once we'd made it to the top of the mountain, we began our descent. It was fast, but I felt safe with Cotton. Even back then, I trusted him with my life and knew he'd never let anything happen to me. It took almost forty-five minutes for us to reach our final destination, and it was worth every second.

As soon as he put the truck in park, he got out and walked over, quickly opening my door. He took a hold of my hand and helped me down out of the truck, quickly leading me toward an old dirt path. I'd been on several trails at the Cape, but never like the secluded trail Cotton was leading me down. The path was winding and steep, and covered with fallen leaves and branches, and I was captivated by Cotton's smile as he rushed us toward our destination, dodging and jumping over any obstacles that blocked our way. We were like two kids searching for lost treasure on a deserted island, both of us excited by the thrill of the hunt. The path was less than a mile long and ended abruptly at the edge of the Pacific Ocean. The view was spectacular. We were just a few steps away from the crystal clear water when Cotton reached for me, wrapping his arms around my waist so I wouldn't fall.

"Whoa," he laughed. "It's farther down than it looks."

I looked out at the rolling waves and crystal clear water, and I couldn't wait to put my feet in. "Can we get down there?" I asked.

"Yeah," he answered with a devilish grin. "But it isn't exactly easy. Are you up for the challenge?"

"Are you doubting me, Cotton?" I asked as I placed my hands on my hips.

"Not for a minute."

He took a few steps forward and then eased himself down onto a large rock. As soon as he had his footing, he reached out his hand and helped me down. It took several tricky moves before we made it safely down from the cliff. When I was done brushing the dirt from my shorts, I looked up to him and said, "You've done that a time or two, haven't you?"

"A time or two."

The waves were too rough for a swim, so I just took off my tennis shoes and walked along the edge of the water. When he walked up next to me, I asked, "Do you come out here often?"

"I used to when I was a kid. My brothers and I would spend most of our summers out here exploring. I just don't have the time to come down much anymore."

"It's really beautiful. I can see why you like it."

"My dad used to love it out here. We'd pack a picnic and spend the entire day collecting rocks and shells..." his voice trailed off.

I placed my hand on his shoulder, trying to comfort him in some way, and said, "Sounds like a really nice memory."

He nodded, then quietly continued down the shoreline. When he came across a black rock, he knelt down and picked it up. He reached for my hand and placed it in my palm as he smiled and said, "My mother used to say the black ones were good luck, but I've always been a fan of the white ones. They're harder to find."

I ran the tip of my finger over the smooth surface and

said, "They are really pretty. I'm not sure which one I'd like best."

"Then we'll get some of both." We spent the next hour searching for the beautiful black and white rocks Cotton used to collect as a kid. By the time the sun started to set, we'd gathered quite a collection.

I looked down at our pile and said, "You were right. The white ones are amazing."

"I'm glad you like them," Cotton smiled. He looked back at the sunset and said, "We'd better get going. You think you can make the climb back up?"

"Yeah," I answered, feeling a little disappointed we were already leaving.

Once we made it to the top, Cotton said, "You're going to want to see this."

I followed him over to a large, flat rock that rested on the edge of the cliff and sat down next to him. I was caught off-guard when he reached over and pulled me closer to him. I nestled into his side and rested my head on his shoulder. We watched in silence as the sun set over the ocean, making the sky turn beautiful shades of pink and deep orange.

I looked over to him, noticing the sparkle in his eyes as he watched the sun fade from the sky, and said, "It's really beautiful, Cotton."

"I thought you might like it. It's almost as beautiful as…" he started, but stopped himself.

I wanted him to finish that sentence, but decided not to push and said, "I'm glad you brought me here. Maybe I can show you my special place sometime."

"Yeah? Where's your special place?"

"I know it sounds a little silly, but I always loved my grandmother's backyard. It overlooks the ocean, and she has this unbelievable tree that sits right off to the edge of her yard. It's so tall, seems to go for miles, and I loved to climb as high as I could before my dad would fuss at me and make me come down. And there was this swing… I guess my place pales in comparison to yours."

"I think it sounds pretty amazing," he smiled. Darkness slowly began to cascade around us as the sun set, and my heart sank when I realized our time together was about to end. As expected, he turned to me and said, "It's time to head back."

"Okay."

"Maybe next time I'll take you to one of the caves we've found. It's on the other side of the Cape, and you'll need some boots," he smiled, and just the thought of being alone with him again excited me.

"I'd like that."

He stepped closer, really close, then rested his hands on my hips as he pulled me over to him. My mind began to race with a million thoughts as he lowered his lips to mine, kissing me for the very first time. I wanted to hold him there, savor the moment, but before things became heated, he pulled back and studied my face for just a moment. After several seconds, he finally said, "You're really something, Cass."

I was remembering the thrill I got from that first stolen kiss when Henley thumped my arm and said, "*Hey*. Don't get your panties in a twist. You know I was just teasing. I think Cotton is awesome. *Really*. I can see why you're crazy about him."

"Um hmm," I grumbled.

"Seriously. I think you two are great together. I'm just ready for y'all to get on with it. You know? It's time for him to throw you over his shoulder and claim you as his woman," she laughed. She sat there, staring at me for a second, and when I didn't say anything, she asked, "Seriously… are you going to tell me what happened when he took you to the back or what?" Heat rushed to my face the second I thought back to what he'd said earlier, and the second Henley noticed, she leaned forward and smiled as she said, "Never mind. You don't have to say a word. It's written all over you face."

"Whatever. No, it's not," I said defensively.

"You're blushing, Cass. I don't know if I've ever even seen you blush before," she mocked. "So I guess it went well."

"Yeah, you could say that," I told her as I tried to suppress my smile, but it was no use. I couldn't remember when I'd been so relieved, and there was no point in trying to hide it. Before I could say anything more, Henley's attention was drawn to the end of the bar. Even though my back was to him, I didn't have to look to know it was Cotton standing there. I could feel the heat of his stare against my skin.

Henley confirmed the feeling when she said, "Well, speak of the devil."

I leaned in toward her and whispered, "Okay, Henley. This is where you *don't* act like your usual self. Rein that shit in when it comes to Cotton. *Seriously.*"

"Who, me? I don't know *what* you are talking about," she laughed.

When I turned to look at Cotton, I could see the same look of lust in his eyes I'd seen earlier. Damn. I would never get tired of that look. I took a deep breath and tried to settle myself before heading toward him. I'd only taken a few steps when Henley said, "You kids have fun."

After giving her a warning look, I walked over to Cotton and asked, "Everything okay?"

"Better now," he growled as his eyes slowly roamed over my body, causing a slight quiver between my legs. He looked toward the end of the bar and asked, "How's Henley hanging in?"

"The lockdown is getting to her a little bit."

He smiled and said, "I'd say it's getting to us all. Hopefully, things will get back to normal soon."

"That'd be awesome. I could use a day away from all the testosterone," I laughed.

His eyes dropped to my mouth as he teased, "Too much testosterone?"

"Oh yeah… there's only so much a girl can

take. It's like running a daycare around here sometimes. You've gotta admit… your boys are messy and the hallways smell like feet." His head fell back as his laughter rumbled through his chest. I couldn't help but smile. I loved seeing him laugh. For just a brief moment, it looked like the weight of the world had fallen from his shoulders.

Still smiling, he looked back over to me and said, "Yeah, the bathrooms can get pretty bad."

"Bad? Oh no… they are worse than bad! I'm scared to even walk in there!"

"I'm not sure if you've noticed, but I'm pretty sure there's something growing in the back of the refrigerator. It's green, and I think it might have even waved at me."

"Hold up… you just left it there?" When he nodded, I fussed, "Cotton, that's so gross! You're just as bad as the rest of them!"

"Not even going to try to deny it," he smiled.

Shaking my head, I told him, "You are too much!"

He didn't respond. He just sat there, quietly staring at me, making me wonder what he was thinking. I leaned closer to him, placing my elbows on the bar as I flirted, "You know… when I see that look, I always wonder if I should be nervous or really, really turned on."

With a wicked grin, he said, "Only one way to find out." He didn't wait for my response.

Instead, his warm, strong hand took a hold of mine, and he led me down the hall. I followed him inside his room, feeling my heart beat rapidly against my chest as I waited for him to approach me. He slowly stalked over to me, closing the space between us, while I stood there, unable to take my eyes off of him. I wanted him, all of him… now and forever, and it terrified me. I looked up at him, seeing the passion that lay behind those beautiful dark brown eyes, and my pulse pounded harder, roaring in my ears as I waited for him to take that last step. And then it happened. He was standing in front of me, so close I could feel the heat of his breath against my flesh, and before I could even react, he brought his hands to my face, holding me steady as he lowered his mouth to mine. His intoxicating scent, the subtle mix of cologne and leather, surrounded me, only intensifying my arousal. His tongue explored my mouth, slow and deep, making every cell in my body fill with need. Maybe it was because he'd finally admitted his feelings, but I'd never felt so much from just one kiss. I knew then that I'd never feel the same about any other man.

I was so lost in the moment that I didn't even notice he'd unfastened the buttons of my skirt until it dropped to the floor. He pushed his hips into mine, revealing his growing erection as the bulging denim ground against my center. My heart was beating out of control. Everything was happening so fast, but it felt like a dream, every detail playing out in slow motion. I wanted it so much. I wanted *him* so much, and I couldn't wait a moment longer. Groaning into his mouth, I eagerly unbuckled his belt and released him from his jeans. I reached for him, my fingertips gently brushing across his swollen shaft. I heard him take in a deep breath as he took hold of the hem of my sweater and pulled it over my head. He began kissing me again as he reached behind me to remove my lace bra.

Once it hit the floor, his eyes dropped to my breasts, and he breathed, "So damn perfect." He let out a low growl as he reached for my ass, lifting me up close to him.

"Cotton…," I whispered as I wrapped my legs around his waist. He carried me over to the bed, laying me flat on my back. As soon as he removed my boots and his, he covered me with the warmth of his body. He gently took my nipple in his mouth, taking his time as he nipped at my sensitive skin. A moan permeated the room as I arched my back, pressing my breasts toward him. The bristles of his two-day old beard brushed against my skin when he lowered his mouth to the curves of my stomach, licking and nipping my flesh as he settled himself between my legs. When his teeth raked across my panties, I groaned out with pleasure. With one quick jerk, he ripped them from my waist, making my legs quiver as his hand moved between my thighs. His fingers circled my clit, while he continued to torment me with his mouth. When his fingers entered me, I rocked my hips against his hand, encouraging him to move faster, but it made no difference. He was the one in command of my body, and he was determined to make me shatter with his touch. My clit throbbed with the need for release, causing me to whimper as my body tensed and filled with heat. When the sensation grew to be more than I could bear, I screamed out with pleasure, calling out Cotton's name over and over as my orgasm exploded, rocking me to my very core. My chest heaved as I struggled to catch my breath.

"You're even more beautiful when you cum," he rasped as he began to pull his shirt over his head, exposing the defined muscles of his bare chest. Unable to resist the temptation, my fingers quickly started to roam over the lines of his colorful ink… my god, he was gorgeous.

As I continued to explore him with my hand, I slowly eased up on my knees, letting my eyes soak in the beauty of his body. When I caught sight of his throbbing erection, I couldn't resist the temptation to touch him. I eagerly reached out for him, taking him in my hand, then slowly started to stroke him. Without the least bit of resistance, he lowered his back to the mattress. I felt him grow even harder as I moved my hand up and down his long, thick shaft. His eyes closed and he groaned as I leaned forward, gently licking the tip of his cock.

"Fuck, you make me so hard," he growled.

"Hmm," I moaned and opened my mouth wider. He tangled his hands in my hair, silently begging me for more as I took him in my mouth as far as I could. When he tilted his head back and moaned my name, I became even more aroused. I loved seeing him like this, completely lost in the pleasure I was giving him. A low rumble worked its way through his chest when I started to move faster, licking and sucking his cock, making him struggle to maintain control. With deep satisfaction, I listened to his sharp breaths and watched the torment on his face until his eyes suddenly opened and locked on mine.

"Love your mouth, Cass, but I need inside of you... now," he growled.

When he reached for his jeans, I whispered, "Please don't. Not this time... I'm on the shot. I want to feel you... all of you."

I lay back on the bed, and without hesitation, he settled himself between my legs. He looked down at my body with desire so intense I could feel the heat of his gaze burn against my skin. My body tingled with lust when he teased my entrance with his cock, bringing me to the point of pure agony before he drove deep inside me in one swift thrust. He filled me, completely. A needful moan vibrated through his chest as he gazed down upon my naked body. He lowered his face to my neck, the bristles of his beard tickling against my skin as he nipped and sucked along the contours of my neck. Once he knew I'd adjusted to him, he withdrew slowly, deliberately, causing chills to run down my spine as I waited for him to enter me again. He drove deeper inside me as I tightened around him, and a deep moan vibrated through his chest as he began to increase his pace. I moved with him; our rhythm was flawless, like our bodies had been made for each other. As we continued to move together, pleasure crashed through me like a tidal wave. My body tensed from the exquisite agony of another build, causing him to lose all control. He took me harder, faster, forcing me closer to the edge.

"I want to feel you come undone, Cass," he whispered. I felt his breath against my neck as his teeth raked against my skin.

He continued to whisper in my ear, but I didn't understand him. I was too far gone. My body trembled with anticipation as he slid one hand down between our bodies. As soon as he brushed his thumb over my swollen clit, I was gone. I'd lost all sense of control, and there was nothing I could do but scream out my pleasure when my body exploded and jolted around him. I raked my nails across his back as I clamped down around him, urging him to give in to his release. Unable to contain his climax any longer, Cotton's body tensed, and he drove into me one last time, holding himself deep inside me as he found his release.

While he still remained inside me, his body rested on top of mine, and I could feel the thunder of his heartbeat pulse against my chest. I loved having the weight of his body pressed against mine and groaned with displeasure when he rolled to the side, collapsing with exhaustion onto the bed. Missing his warmth, I curled up next to him, resting my head on his shoulder. I lay there quietly as I waited for the tremors in my body to settle. We'd never had sex like that before: possessive, hungry, and filled with need and heat. It was like Cotton wanted to own my body, and I couldn't get enough of it. I wanted him, all of him, and as I listened to his breathing begin to slow, I felt a contentment I'd never felt before. He gave me a light squeeze, pulling me from my thoughts.

A sexy grin spread across his face as he said, "Definitely the best part of my day."

"Mine, too," I laughed, feeling a warmth in my heart like I'd never known.

Chapter 5

COTTON

A FIRE BURNED deep inside me, one fueled by the need to protect what was mine. When things were good with my family and my brothers, the fire would simmer, low and dim, and I wouldn't even know it was there. But when there was trouble, or when my family was threatened, the fire would rage inside me like a beast clawing its way out of a cage. Cass brought a different fuel to my flame. My need for her burned deep within me, and after spending the night with her, I knew I'd never get enough of her. She'd fallen asleep in my arms, and I couldn't remember a night when I'd slept so soundly. She was so warm and soft, and I would have liked nothing more than to spend the entire day tangled in the sheets with her. Unfortunately, fate had other plans. Fuck fate. Fuck fate and the goddamn horse she rode in on.

"Cotton," Maverick called as he banged on

my door. I rolled over to check the clock on my nightstand and saw it was only eight in the morning—too damn early for anyone to be knocking at my door.

"Yeah?" I grumbled.

"There's someone here to see you."

"You gonna tell me who?" I snapped.

"Some woman. Says she's a friend of yours," Maverick replied. After a short pause, he said, "Her name is Sara Locke. Said she's come all the way from Alaska."

Fuck. The sound of her name was like a punch to the gut, and even though I hadn't seen her or heard from her in almost twenty-five years, I could still see a perfect image of her face when I closed my eyes. We had history, but that time had come and gone. So why had she come after all this time? What was so damn important she'd come to my club, looking for me? Whatever it was, I had a feeling it wasn't good.

"I'll be out in a minute," I told him as I pulled myself out of bed. With Cassidy still sleeping soundly, I headed to the bathroom to take a quick shower. When I came back out, Cass was awake and propped up on her elbows, giving me a questioning look. Unable to resist temptation, I dropped my towel to the floor and waited as the expression on her face quickly changed. I loved watching her eyes instantly fill with lust, like she could never get enough of me.

With a mischievous smile, she fussed, "You did that on purpose."

"Did what?" I taunted as I reached for my jeans. She sat there, watching me appreciatively as I pulled them up over my hips.

"You know what," she said playfully. "You're just a tease."

As I pulled my t-shirt over my head, I said, "You're the tease, sweetheart. Lying there, wearing nothing but the smile I put on your face, making it hard as hell to walk out of this room." I reached for my boots and said, "Unfortunately for me, I've got some things I've got to tend to. Might be awhile."

"I'd say that's unfortunate for both of us, but we'll have time for that later. I've got tons to do today too. I'll catch you later when you're done."

After kissing her long and hard, I headed out to find Maverick. I wanted to see if he had any idea why Sara had come looking for me. I found him in the kitchen, talking to Guardrail, and as soon as I walked into the room, Maverick turned to me and said, "She's waiting in the bar."

"Did she say what she wanted?"

"I asked, but she said she'd explain everything to you," Maverick answered.

"Well, I'd say whatever it is, it can't be good. It's been too fucking long, and she wouldn't come all the way from Alaska just to catch up on old times," Guardrail clipped.

Guardrail was there when Sara left for college. He'd just patched in around the time her father was killed by a member of a rival club. Like the rest of us, he was there to witness the fallout between her mother and the club. It wasn't good. Needing someone to blame, her mother cut ties with everyone involved with the club and pushed her daughter to do the same. She wanted Sara to start a life outside of the Satan's Fury MC, so she sent her off to college in another state, making her leave everything she cared about behind. Knowing in the end it was for the best thing for Sara, I never tried to stop her. She was beyond brilliant and had a talent with technology like I'd never seen. Hell, even Big Mike would have trouble going up against her, and I didn't feel right holding her back, preventing her from being everything she could be. When I heard about her success in college and later with her own security firm, I knew it'd been the right decision. That didn't mean it was easy. Hell, it damn near broke me to see her go, and Guardrail knew it.

I ran my hand down the back of my neck, trying to ease some of the building tension, and said, "You two stay close. I need to talk to you about what Big found last night when I finish up with her."

Just before I turned to leave, Maverick said, "We'll be here."

"Cotton," Guardrail called out.

I turned back to him and said, "Yeah?"

"Be prepared, brother. She's was a beauty before, but now... she's a total knockout," he warned.

Trying to ignore the gnawing feeling in the pit of my stomach, I turned and headed for the bar. When I walked in, Sara was sitting with her back to me. She was looking down at her phone, completely focused on the screen, and didn't even realize I was standing behind her. Guardrail was right. She'd grown into a beautiful woman. She was still the same Sara, but there was an elegance to her that hadn't been there before. Her chestnut hair was shorter than I remembered, cut in some trendy style that rested just below her shoulders. It suited her, just like the dark denim jacket and black leggings she was wearing. I cleared my throat as I sat down beside her, drawing her attention to me. When she finally turned to face me, a thousand memories came rushing back, slamming me right in the gut, and I had to fight the urge to turn away. Those damn eyes, so fucking blue you'd think they were plucked straight from the sky, were staring at me with such intensity I almost lost my breath.

"Hey," she said softly. "It's been a long time."

"Yeah. Too long," I clipped. I took a deep breath as I tried to sort through the blur of thoughts racing through my head. Fuck. I wanted to slam my fist on the counter and yell at her, releasing all of the pent-up feelings raging inside me. I wanted an explanation. I deserved to know why she hadn't contacted me, not even once over the past twenty-five years. The only way I knew anything about what was going on in her life was Doc. Sara's mother trusted him and confided in him from time to time, telling him Sara had gotten married and then divorced when her piece of shit husband cheated on her. But all that happened years ago. I wanted to know what had made her come back now, what was so damn important that she'd come to me after so much time had passed. But I couldn't do it. She was Sara, the girl who stole my heart when I was a kid. She looked like the same girl, sounded the same... even smelled the same. I inhaled, and the familiar scent of her Channel No. 5 triggered an unwanted memory, making it difficult to even look at her. I cleared my throat and asked, "What the hell are you doing here, Sara?"

"I... umm..." she stammered. Her back stiffened with resolve as she continued, "I came because I needed to talk to you."

"Ok. Then talk."

"Don't be like that, Cotton. It was hard enough to come here like this at all. I don't need you giving me a hard time on top of it." She paused for a moment, then continued, "I know I should've come sooner. I thought about it a hundred times, but always talked myself out of it."

"It's been twenty-five years, Sara. Twenty-five fucking years, and not so much as a damn phone call."

"I know, Cotton. At first it was just too hard. I missed you so much, and I knew talking to you would only make it harder. Then, after so much time passed… I don't know. I guess I just lost the nerve to pick up the phone. Figured you wouldn't want to talk to me, much less see me," she explained.

"That's crazy, Sara. You were always welcome here. Always. I know things were rough when your dad died. It was rough on all of us, but even after you and your mother left, we've always considered you both to be family. Nothing changed that."

"I know, Cotton, but Mom… she really lost it after Dad died. I'd never seen her like that before, and honestly, she hasn't been the same since." She sighed as she recalled the memory, concern filling her eyes. After a brief pause, she continued, "You know, she moved back here a couple of years ago when Aunt Clara got sick."

"Yeah. We've been keeping an eye on her."

"I knew you would, Cotton. I appreciate it more than you know. Even though she wouldn't like it, it's helped me to know the club would always be there for her," she smiled sincerely. "With work, I haven't been able to visit her as much as I would like, but she seems happy being with her sister."

"Is she the reason why you're here now, or is there something else?" I finally asked.

The blood quickly drained from her face as she said, "No, Cotton. My visit has nothing to do with my mother. I've come because of Derek."

The sound of his name coming from her mouth caught me by surprise. I couldn't rationalize it in my head, so I growled, "What about *Derek*?"

"It's a long story, but the short version of it is… I think he's stalking me again, but this time it's different. This time, I'm worried he might try to kill me."

"Tell me what's happened, Sara. I need to know everything," I ordered.

"It started with strange things happening around my house and work. Things like weird gifts left on my doorstep or on my car and strange phone calls in the middle of the night. Then, almost two months ago, I saw him for the first time. I was making a coffee run for the team and ran into him at the checkout counter. I was surprised to see him in Anchorage, but at the time, I didn't make much of it. I mean, it seemed simple enough, until I ran into him again a couple of days later at my favorite diner. Even then,

I knew it could've been a coincidence, but I never liked Derek. After what happened all those years ago, I definitely never trusted the guy. When I asked him about it, he just tried to play it off like it was nothing, but something didn't feel right."

"Did he threaten you?" I asked after I finally stopped pacing and sat back down beside her.

I reached into my pocket and grabbed a cigarette, quickly lighting it, as she said, "No. He was all smiles and charms the first few times we ran into each other. He even had the nerve to ask me out on a date. Promised to show me a good time, but when I blew him off, things started to escalate. Every time I turned around, he was there, and it was starting to get to me. He was flat out stalking me, so I decided to take matters into my own hands—turn the tables on him. I had Seth, my partner at the firm, put a GPS tracker on his bike. I was able to use that to keep an eye on him... to know whenever he was close. My guys were even able to find his warehouse and got intel on some of the guys he was running with. He didn't make it easy on us though. He always covered his tracks, changing out burners and even changing his name. Then, two weeks ago, he vanished. Disappeared without a trace and took most of his crew with him."

"You still haven't told me why you think he's trying to kill you, Sara," I pushed.

"He came back."

She reached for her phone and pulled up one of her pictures. Her hand was trembling as she turned the screen to me, showing me a picture of her sleeping soundly in her bed. At first, it didn't register what the picture meant. There was no message. No one standing in the background, just her lying there, sleeping. Then it hit me. Sara was home alone, and someone had come into her house while she was sleeping and took the picture. Fuck.

"What kind of person would do something like that? He's insane, Cotton. He always has been. I can't believe he was actually in my house, standing right next to my bed while I was sleeping. I can't shake it. It's all I can think about."

"Are you sure he's the one who took the picture?"

"Oh, it was him. There's no doubt. Something woke me up, and the first thing I noticed was my phone. The screen was lit up, and when I checked it, I found that picture of me. I rushed out of bed and went straight to my laptop to check the security footage of the house, and that's when I saw Derek. He was right there by my bed, and he wasn't alone. Joe Delaney was standing next to him while he smiled at the security camera. He's a hacker, one of the best. The FBI has been trying to track him down for months. He's the one who got Derek inside the house without setting off my alarm. After seeing that footage, I couldn't stay in that house a minute longer. I packed my bags and headed here."

"I'll take care of it," I promised. I'm not sure what triggered it, maybe it was part of his plan for revenge or maybe it was just seeing her again that did it, but Derek's obsession with Sara was back. Whatever the reason, I'd have to do whatever I could to protect her.

She sighed with relief and said, "I was hoping you'd say that."

"I'm going to need everything you've got on him and his crew."

"Most of it's on my computer, but I can get Seth from work to send the rest."

"Gonna need you to stay here till we get this thing sorted."

A nervous grin crossed her face as she said, "I guess it's pointless for me to say I can stay at mom's."

"You'll be safer here," I told her. I decided to wait until our meet with Big Mike to fill her in on Derek's attack on the club. I'd let her get settled first and explain everything when she gave us her intel on Derek. "I've gotta take care of a few things. I'll get one of the girls to help you get settled."

"I don't need a babysitter, Cotton. Just tell me which room, and I'll take care of the rest."

"The last two rooms in the left wing are open. Don't get too comfortable. We'll be leaving for Anchorage as soon as I get things sorted," I told her as I stood to leave.

"Okay," she agreed. She stood up and quickly wrapped her arms around my neck. "Thanks, Cotton. It's really good to see you."

"Good to see you too," I told her then gently pulled free from her embrace and headed for the door. Even though I knew Guardrail and Maverick were waiting to hear what was going on, I needed a minute to myself to decompress. I went straight to my office and shut the door behind me, trying to shut out all the noise in my head. I sat down at my desk and had just reached for a cigarette when there was a knock at the door.

"Yeah?"

Guardrail slowly eased the door open, and I nodded for him to enter. He took a seat in front of my desk and said, "So, I just saw Sara bringing her bags down the hall. What the hell is that all about? Is she really staying here?"

"Yeah," I told him as I lit my cigarette. "For now."

He cleared his throat and asked, "You good? Couldn't have been easy to see her after all this time."

"Yeah, I'm good, but things just took a turn, brother. We're going to need to head to Anchorage. The sooner, the better."

"Anchorage?" he questioned. "Why the hell are we going to Alaska?"

"Because Derek's there, and we're going after him. Sara managed to get some intel on him before he pulled his stunt last night."

His eyebrows furrowed as he asked, "What stunt?"

"The asshole broke into her house last night, and it took some maneuvering, brother. He got past her high tech security system. Even took a fucking picture of her sleeping and used her phone to take it."

"Damn. Why didn't he just kill her while he had the chance?"

"We both know why. Sara has been gone a long time, but she's still family – our family. He knows I wouldn't let anything happen to her. He wants me to come after him, and that's exactly what I'm going to do."

Chapter 6

CASS

★

AFTER COTTON LEFT, I couldn't go back to sleep. Every time I rolled over and smelled his scent on the pillows, my mind would start racing a mile a minute. I tossed and turned, and finally decided it was pointless. There was no way I was going back to sleep, so I got up and headed for the kitchen. I decided to make the guys some breakfast, and just as I started to heat the sausage, Clutch walked in, wearing his cut with a pair of beat-up, old blue jeans. His green eyes sparkled when he smiled, making it irresistible not to smile right back at him. He sauntered over to me and leaned against the stove, and as soon as he looked up at me, I could tell he was going to hit me up for something. I didn't know why he even tried being slick. He'd never been very good at hiding anything from me.

"Hey, beautiful. You need any help with that?" he asked playfully.

"I'm good. Thanks, though."

"It smells *great*," he smiled.

I turned to face him, pointing the spatula at his chest, and asked, "I know you're up to something. Just tell me. What do you want this time?" Of all the brothers at the club, we got along the best. He was always in a great mood and never failed to make me smile.

He cocked his head to the side and said, "Who, me? I don't want anything."

"Spill it," I told him as I poked him in the chest with the spatula.

"Okay, I might need a little help with something," he admitted. He shrugged his shoulders and said, "I mean, I could do it by myself, but I'm *wounded*."

"Oh, please. Are you still milking that?" I teased. I'd been fussing at him for days to take it easy. His arm was wrapped up in a sling, and he'd barely started to get his color back. He'd gotten shot a week ago when another club broke into Wren's house and kidnapped her. Typical Clutch, he was more upset over them getting Wren than he ever was about being shot. I don't know if he will ever forgive himself for letting them get past him.

He gave me a pathetic look and said, "That hurts, Cass. I've been shot. Twice. I almost died."

I was actually starting to feel guilty about giv-

COTTON

ing him a hard time until he started laughing. "You're an *ass*," I told him as I rolled my eyes.

"Yeah, but you love me," he taunted.

"Are you going to tell me what you need help with, or am I supposed to guess? No, wait! Let me guess. It's something for one of your *many, many* girlfriends, or you need me to do your laundry again."

"I've only asked you to do my laundry once," he heckled.

"Only because you didn't like my fabric softener."

"I smelled like lilacs, Cass. No guy should smell like fucking lilacs," he fussed.

I couldn't stop myself from laughing. I remembered adding several extra sheets to the dryer just to make sure the scent would be strong enough to last, and it did... for days. I loved it. My entire apartment smelled like lilacs. Clutch wasn't a fan.

"So if it isn't laundry, it must be something about a girl."

"No... well, maybe later. Right now, I need your help with Dusty. He wants me to help him with a project, but I don't even know where to start."

"What kind of project?"

"He's gotta make a model of the Solar System for his science class. And it's gotta have all the bells and whistles. Full on epic project, better than anything they've ever seen before."

"And he asked *you* to help him with that?"

"Of course, he did. I'm the best."

"Okay, Mr. Arts and Crafts. When is the project due?" I asked.

"Tomorrow," he answered with a grimace. "He asked me to help a few weeks ago, and I kinda forgot."

"Clutch!" I scolded. "How are we supposed to get this done in a day?"

"I don't know. That's why I'm asking you."

"Let me finish this up, and then I'll make a list of things we're going to need. Maybe you can get Scooter to make a run for us."

"Thanks, Cass. I knew I could count on you. I'll go see if I can round up Scooter," Clutch said as he grabbed a piece of cooked sausage off the skillet and turned to leave.

I quickly finished putting together the sausage and biscuits and turned off the stove. Once I had everything put on the table, I got out a piece of paper and started my shopping list. I was still writing when Dusty walked in.

"Hey, Cass-dy," he smiled and reached for a biscuit. "Me and Clutch are gonna do my project today."

"Clutch was telling me about that. It's going to be awesome."

"It's the Solar System and it's gonna have lights," he said proudly.

"Lights!" I gasped. Clutch never mentioned he promised Dusty lights.

"Yep. It's going to be ep-ic," he laughed.

The smile on his face was contagious, and in a matter of seconds, I found myself feeling just as excited as he was about his not-so-little science project. "Yes, it's definitely going to be epic."

"Where's Clutch?" he asked as he took a big bite of his biscuit.

"He'll be back in a minute. He's got to get a few things together before you can start your project."

"Okay."

"When I was a kid, I really loved doing projects like this. Would you mind if I helped a little?"

"Yeah. That'd be cool," he answered.

"Awesome. I'll let you know when he gets back so we can get started," I offered.

"Okeydokey. I'm gonna go play video games with Wy-it," he shouted as he walked out of the kitchen.

I finished up my very detailed list and gave it to Scooter and Clutch, giving them both explicit directions to buy exactly what was on the list. When they returned, they had me follow them into the TV room where Clutch had set up a table for us to work on. When Clutch dumped everything out of the table, I was completely flabbergasted. They'd done what I asked, but they'd also bought a ton of crap we'd never be able to use.

Astounded, I placed my hand on my forehead and asked, "Exactly *why* do we need balloons and confetti?"

"I told you it was going to be epic," Clutch laughed.

"Just so we're clear, I told him he didn't need all this stuff," Scooter said, shaking his head.

"Yeah, I think you may have gone a little overboard here, Clutch," I warned.

"Nah, it's going to be awesome. Where's Dusty?" Clutch asked.

"He's in his room, playing video games with Wyatt."

Scooter headed for the door and said, "I'll go get him while you guys get everything set up."

"Thanks, man," Clutch told him as he started organizing the huge pile of supplies he'd bought. I stood there and watched in amazement as he sorted through all the things he'd purchased. He'd finally gotten everything into place when Dusty walked in. When he saw all the goodies, he rushed over to us and looked at all the different-colored balls and paints spread out on the table.

"You ready to get busy?" Clutch asked him.

"Yep."

"Why don't you help Cass paint the sun?" he suggested.

"Okay," he said, reaching for the paint brush. His chubby, little fingers wrapped around the brush and a wide smile spread across his face as he started painting. He took his time, and when he was done, he started on the blue planets. It'd only been a few minutes when he got bored with the paints and started in with the questions.

"Where are the lights?"

"They're still in the box. We'll put those on last," Clutch told him as he glued one of the planets on the box.

"Where we gonna put 'em?"

"They'll go on the back, so they'll look like stars when we turn them on," Clutch explained.

"Can I blow up a balloon?" he asked.

"They're all yours, buddy," Clutch smiled.

Dusty grabbed a handful of balloons and started blowing them up, one right after the other. Clutch quickly realized Dusty was more interested in playing with all the junk he'd bought instead of actually working on the project. It'd only been fifteen minutes or so when Dusty asked me, "Can I take a balloon to Wyatt?"

"Sure, honey. We'll let the paint dry, and we can finish this up later," I told him, and the minute he got the okay to leave, he grabbed his balloons and he was gone.

We continued to work on the project, and when everything was almost finished, Clutch turned to me and said, "Thanks for helping me with this, Cass. I wouldn't have been able to do it without you."

"I don't know about that, but it does look pretty amazing."

"It does, doesn't it?" he said proudly.

"It does. You did good. I'm sure Dallas will appreciate it, too. She's been working so much with her new job, and she hates not being able to spend as much time with Dusty. I'm sure it means a lot to her," I told him while I started to clean up the mess we'd made.

"Just glad I could do something to help. I've gotta check in with Guardrail. Just leave the rest, and Dusty and I will finish it up later."

"Okay. Just give me a shout if you need me," I told him as I looked down at my hands and clothes. I was covered in paint and glue, so I decided it was time for a hot shower.

When I got to my room, I immediately headed for the bathroom and turned on the hot water. I stepped into the shower and methodically started scrubbing away all the dried paint and glue from my fingernails. It was the first time I'd been alone since my night with Cotton, and I finally had time to let everything that had happened sink in. An involuntary smile crossed my face when I thought about our night together. He'd taken that step, and I couldn't remember a time when I'd ever been this happy. He was different from any man I'd ever known, and I'd often wondered why I felt such a pull to him. It didn't hurt I found him to be devastatingly handsome, but it was so much more than that. Maybe it was the fact he was older, more mature and confident than men my age. Or maybe it was his loyalty to his family, always putting them before himself. It was everything about him. It was all the little things he'd do or say that made me fall for him, like watching raindrops fall one by one, never realizing I was about to be caught in a storm.

Chapter 7

COTTON

AFTER BIG MIKE walked Guardrail and me through all the information Sara had uncovered about Derek, I called church so we could discuss our next move. We needed to make our move before Derek had time to build his resources. We decided to leave for Anchorage first thing in the morning. Driving thirty-eight hours in the bitter cold wasn't an option, so Big booked flights for me, Stitch, Maverick, and Sara. I wanted extra eyes on the club while we were gone, so I put in a call to Rip. He agreed that his club, the Forsaken Saints, would secure our territory while we were gone, ensuring that no one entered the area without our knowledge. Knowing that Derek's threat against the club was no longer imminent, we decided to lift the lockdown, but all members were expected to be on high alert. It was important for all of us to keep our families under close watch.

Once the meeting dismissed, I headed over to my mother's loft to let her know I would be leaving. Over the years, she'd become accustomed to the club life, but that didn't mean she was happy about it. I wanted her to be comfortable whenever she was forced to join our lockdowns, so I made her a small apartment over the main garage, giving her a space of her own whenever she was at the club. When I walked in, she was sitting on her sofa, drinking a cup of coffee. She watched quietly as I poured myself a cup and joined her in the living room.

Sensing the tension I was carrying, she asked, "Hey, sweetheart. Is everything okay?"

"Sara's here."

"It's been a long time since I've heard that name. I take it she's doing well," she huffed as she placed her cup of coffee down on the table and crossed her arms. I could see she wasn't happy Sara had returned. When she left for college, mom wanted me to go with her and hated the fact I had no interest in following her. She'd always wanted my brothers and me to go to college and start lives outside of the club, and even though she's seen that we've had a good life, she's always wanted more for us. Sara had gotten out, and a part of my mother resented her for it.

"She's doing alright, I guess," I answered, hoping she wouldn't push for more.

Without skipping a beat, she smiled and asked, "Has she finally come back to claim her lost love?"

Shaking my head, I answered, "No. That ship sailed a long time ago."

"Are you sure about that? You know, there was a time when you really loved that girl," she asked with regret in her eyes. There was one thing I always knew for certain when it came to my mother, she loved us. She was hard on us, had to be with three boys, but she'd move mountains to make sure we were happy.

"I'm sure. It's all good, so don't worry."

"I'll always worry, Cotton," she cried as she brought her hand up to her chest. "You know, I'm not getting any younger, and all this worrying isn't good for my heart. It sure would make it easier on your old mother if you'd just settle down and have me some grandchildren. Just one or two—enough to keep me distracted." And there it was. She always managed to get it in one way or another.

"You've already got two grandkids, mom," I scolded.

"And they are precious, but they aren't yours," she smiled.

"Ok, I'm working on it," I laughed. "I just came by to let you know we're going out of town for a little while. Joe and Luke will be around if you need anything, and you can go back to the house whenever you're ready."

"Does this mean the trouble you were in is over?" she asked.

"Not exactly, but it'll all be over soon enough."

"Then I'm staying right here till you get back. Besides, I like being close to my boys whenever I can," she smiled.

I stood to leave, but before I could get out the door, Joe came in, and when he saw me standing there, said "Hey, bro. When ya leaving?"

"Early tomorrow morning. Gonna need you to keep an eye on Mom and Cass while we're gone."

"You got it. You sure you don't want me to go with you? Luke can watch over Mom and Cass," he offered.

"No, need you here more. Luke will have his hands full with Katie and the kids," I told him as I walked toward the door. "Guardrail's in charge while we're gone. Let him know if anything comes up."

He nodded as I turned to leave. Before I walked out, I turned to Mom and said, "Joe's got himself a new lady friend. Heard they were an item," I taunted. "Bet he'd be more than happy to give you some grandbabies."

When I shut the door, I heard Joe yell, "Thanks a lot, bro!"

Feeling the need to recharge, I was ready to

lay my eyes on Cass, but it was getting late and I needed to let Sara know we were going to be leaving in the morning. I hated the thought of leaving Cass, but Derek had to be dealt with, the sooner the better.

When I knocked on her door, she called out, "The door's open."

When I walked in, she had her back propped up against the wall and a stack of papers resting in her lap. "Got a minute?"

"Sure. Come on in," she answered and motioned for me to enter.

"Just wanted to let you know we'll be leaving at five-thirty tomorrow morning."

"Okay. I'll be ready." She quickly sifted through the stack of papers, and when she found the page she was looking for, she said, "I've been looking at all the stuff Seth sent over, and I wanted to show you something. Seth has been trying to locate the rest of Derek's men. From security footage, we already knew Joe Delaney made it back, but other than him, we've only been able to locate two of the guys who left with Derek two weeks ago. That means most of the others were killed during their attack on your club."

Typical Sara, she'd managed to put two and two together before I'd even started to explain everything that had happened with Derek. With the information she'd gathered, we'd have no problem locating Derek and putting an end to this whole thing once and for all. "Good. We'll have less to contend with when we get to Anchorage."

"I really appreciate you doing all this," she said softly. "I didn't know who else to turn to."

"Glad you came to me," I smiled. "You've helped us more than you realize." I paused for a moment, thinking about what Doc had told me about her ex, then said, "I'm sorry about you and Ben."

"Nothing to be sorry about, Cotton. It was good for a while, but we grew apart. And it didn't help he slept around," she laughed.

"He didn't know how good he had it," I smiled.

"Guess not. Doesn't matter. I'm over it," she said. She glanced back at the papers in her hand, and asked, "What do you know about Delaney?"

Figuring she was ready to change the subject, I answered, "Not much. Whatcha got?"

We spent the next half hour going over everything she had on Derek's three remaining men. One of the older guys had a connection to another club, while the others were just tagalongs Derek had acquired months earlier. By the time we'd gone over everything she had on them, it was after eleven. When I closed her door behind me, I found Clutch walking down the hall in my direction.

"Late night, Prez?" he smiled as his eyes darted over to Sara's door.

"Tying up some loose ends," I answered. "We're leaving before dawn. Need you to keep an eye on Cass while I'm gone. You gonna be up for that?" Clutch had always been my go-to guy, but he was still healing and I needed his word he could handle her.

"I'm up for it. Anything you need, Prez."

"Good. If you need anything, you know how to reach me."

He gave me a quick chin lift and headed to his room. When he shut his door, I set out to find Cass. I thought I'd find her in the bar, but with the lockdown lifted, the place was completely deserted. Coming up empty-handed, I headed to my room, hoping to find her waiting for me in my bed. Regrettably, I found both empty. Fuck. I'd been waiting all day to see her, *all fucking day*, and I wasn't going to wait a second longer. I stormed down the hall, and without even knocking, opened her door. I walked over to her bed, and when I pulled her comforter back, her eyes flashed open.

"Cotton! What are..." she gasped.

Her mouth clamped shut when I leaned over her and quickly lifted her out of bed, cradling her in my arms. She didn't resist; instead, she smiled and rested her head on my shoulder. Damn. That's all it took. With just the feel of her body pressed against mine, the tension I'd been carrying around began to lift from my shoulders. When we got to my room, I kicked the door shut and eased her down onto my bed. I stood over her, crossing my arms as I growled, "I thought you understood."

Her eyebrows furrowed with confusion as she asked, "Understood what?"

"I want you… all of you. Your taste, your smell, the feel of your body next to mine, and I won't spend *one night* in this bed without it."

"I just thought…"

"Tonight, and every night after, I fall asleep with you in my arms," I interrupted. "And when I'm not here, I still want you in **my** bed."

With her eyes locked on mine, she whispered, "Okay."

I pulled off my t-shirt and along with my jeans and boots, tossed it to the floor. Her eyes flickered with appreciation as she watched me crawl into the bed next to her. Once I was settled, she curled up next to me and laid her head on my chest.

With the tips of her fingers, she began to trace the lines of my tattoo as she said, "I couldn't stop thinking about you today."

"Is that right?" I smiled.

"I didn't even realize I was doing it until I caught myself smiling. I guess I do that a lot… probably more than I should," she admitted.

I took her hand in mine and lightly kissed the palm of her hand as I said, "I've thought about you a time or two."

She smiled and said, "Hmmm... A time or two, huh? I must be losing my touch."

"Not a chance," I told her as I ran my fingers through her long hair. "How'd Dusty's project go?"

"You should've seen it. Clutch went all out and bought all kinds of stuff we didn't even need. It was a mess, but Dusty was tickled to death with it."

"I'm sure he was. I would be, too. I used to love doing projects like that, but mine usually involved blowing something up," I laughed.

"Blowing stuff up? I'm sure your mother loved that."

"Yeah, we gave her a run for her money. My brothers and I were always getting into stuff. When Joe discovered what would happen when you put Mentos into a soda bottle, it was a game changer."

She was quiet for a minute, then looked up to me and asked, "What time are you leaving tomorrow?"

"Early. An old friend..." I let out a breath, then continued, "*Sara* needs our help. The sooner we get to Anchorage, the better." The light mood instantly changed as her eyes dropped to my chest and concern washed over her face. I didn't like the thought of leaving her any more than she did, but it was something that had to be done. I brought my hand to her chin, forcing her to look at me, when I said, "I'll be back before you know it."

"I know. It's hard not to worry though, especially when you'll be so far away, and ... just please be careful."

"Always," I told her and dropped my mouth to hers, kissing her long and hard. Her mouth was warm and wet, and all of her little moans and whimpers made my cock ache with need. When she pulled her nightgown over her head, exposing her perfect, round breasts, I was done. I had to have her. I leaned over her and watched the goosebumps rise along her skin as I began to trace the slope of her breast with my fingertips. She was perfect, every damn inch of her, and I was determined to have her... over and over again. I settled myself between her thighs and ran my tongue across the edge of her lace panties, teasing her, tormenting her as she squirmed beneath me. Her scent was intoxicating, and I was overcome with the need to taste her. I slipped her panties down past her ankles while trailing kisses down the thick of her thigh.

I slid my hands under her ass as I lowered my head between her legs and watched as her back arched off of the bed when I brushed my tongue across her clit. Damn. I loved how her body responded instantly to my touch. I couldn't get enough. I continued to lick and suck her clit while easing my fingers deep inside her, finding the spot that drove her wild. I covered her with my mouth, sucking and nipping until her body jolted and bucked beneath me. With the sounds of her moans echoing through the room, I placed my hands on her thighs, holding her in place while I continued to work her over with my mouth. Her taste had my cock throbbing with an uncontrollable need to be inside her, and when I could wait no longer, I quickly removed my boxers and settled myself between her legs.

I placed my mouth close to her ear and whispered, "I don't think I'll ever be able to get enough of you."

Without saying a word, she pressed her lips to mine in a possessive, demanding kiss and wrapped her legs around my waist, pressing my cock against her. There was no doubt she wanted me just as much as I wanted her, and I had every intention of giving her all I had to give. I spent the entire night making love to her, taking my time to burn every inch of her body into my memory. I wanted to remember every moment, every touch, so I'd have some part of her with me while I was gone.

Chapter 8

CASSIDY

MY HAND DRIFTED over to Cotton's side of the bed, longing to touch him one last time before he left, but I was too late. He was gone. The warm spot where he'd once lain was now empty and cold. I brought my knees up to my chest, curling myself into a ball as I tried to hold it together, but it was no use. Once the first tear fell, I was lost. With tears streaming down my cheeks, I reached for his pillow and was immediately hit with his scent. Damn. How could I already miss him? He'd only been gone for a couple of hours, and I was already a complete mess. I had to stop. Trying to pull it together, I sat up in the bed and wiped the tears from my face. I was too strong to just let myself fall apart. I got up and headed down the hall. As soon as I was in my room, I turned on one of Norah Jones' soundtracks and blared it while I took a long, hot shower. Even with the distraction of my favorite song, I couldn't shake the feeling that something was wrong, like something bad was going to happen. It was eating at me, and I had to do something to distract myself from my thoughts. Henley was the best distraction I knew, so I set out to find her.

Since we were no longer under lockdown, most of the families had left, but since Maverick was with Cotton, I knew she'd still be at the club. It was still pretty early, so I decided to try their room first. When I tapped on the door, she yelled, "Give me a minute."

Several minutes passed, but she never came to the door, so I cracked it open and peaked inside. The room was empty, but I heard a commotion in the bathroom. Just as I stepped in the room, she came walking out of the bathroom with a wet rag in her hand, looking like something the cat had dragged in. "What's wrong with you?"

"Stomach bug or something," she groaned. "I must've caught something from one of the kids."

"I thought you were feeling better."

She brushed her hair out of her eyes and said, "I was. I mean… I've been a little tired, but then it hit me again this morning." She sat down on the edge of the bed, looking like she might get sick again, and said, "This sucks."

"How about some saltines and ginger ale?" I

offered.

"I'm fine. Can you just sit here with me for a minute?"

I sat down next to her and placed the palm of my hand on her forehead, checking to see if she had a fever. "I don't think you have a temp."

"I'm okay. Just a little tired," she said, shrugging her shoulders. She paused for a minute, then cocked her head to the side as she brought her hands up to her boobs and lightly squeezed them.

I got tickled watching her and asked, "Feeling yourself up, Sis?"

"My boobs don't feel right. They don't exactly hurt, but they ache or something," she whined.

"Maybe you're about to start your period," I suggested.

Pure terror washed over her face as she asked, "Oh shit. What's today's date?"

"The eighteenth."

"Shit. Shit. Shit!" she shouted as she stood up from the bed and reached for her phone, quickly searching her calendar. "Shit! I was supposed to start on the ninth, and with all this lockdown stuff, I didn't even think about it. Cass, I'm almost two weeks late!"

"Tired, sick to your stomach, and the boob thing… Ah, hell, Henley! We've gotta go get a pregnancy test! Now!" I screeched. I took hand and led her out into the hall, pulling her toward my room, so I could grab my purse and keys.

"Maybe it's just stress," Henley blurted out. "Or the flu... maybe I have the dates wrong. Maybe I had my period and didn't notice it."

"Yeah, like that's possible. There's only one way to find out what's going on," I told her as I headed for the car. Neither of us spoke on the way to the drugstore. We were both lost in our own world of thoughts, and I was too stunned to speak. I was having a hard time believing my little sister could actually be pregnant. When we got inside the store, Henley followed me over to the aisle with all the pregnancy tests. I grabbed several different brands and headed over to the checkout lane.

"Why are you buying so many? Don't we just need one?" Henley asked.

"I don't know. I've never had to do this before. Just figured it was better to be safe than sorry."

Once the clerk gave me my change, I grabbed the bag and we raced out to the car. I started the car, and I was just about to put it in reverse when Henley asked, "Do you think Maverick will be okay with this?"

Surprised by her question, I asked, "What do you mean *okay with this*? Okay with what?"

"What if he doesn't want to have a baby with me? We haven't been together long... and we've never really talked about having kids. And with everything that happened with JW, he may not..." her voice trailed off as tears filled her eyes.

"You've got to be kidding me right now. Maverick loves you, Lee Bug. You're his ol' lady, and if you are having his kid, he's going to be over the moon about it."

"You really think so?"

I placed my hand on her shoulder and said, "No doubt in my mind. You are worrying over nothing. Besides, we don't even know if you are really pregnant yet."

"I hope you're right, because..." she started. "I really want this."

Once we got back to the club, we took our bag of goodies and went straight to Henley's room. She took no time rushing into the bathroom to take the first test. Through the closed door, she yelled, "It says to pee on the stick. What if I pee on my hand?"

"Then you wash your damn hand. Now, hurry up and pee!" I laughed.

"I'm trying. Stop rushing me!" she fussed. A few seconds later, I heard the toilet flush, but Henley didn't open the door.

"Lee Bug?"

"Cass... There's already a plus sign," she murmured. "I'm taking another one." There was a brief moment of silence before I heard her stirring around as she yelled, "Two lines. I got two lines on this one."

I opened the door and found her standing there, staring at the pregnancy tests with a huge smile on her face. Her expression said it all. I rushed over to her, hugging her tightly as I said, "I can't believe this is really happening! I am so happy for you."

She buried her face in my neck as she cried, "I'm going to have a baby. Maverick's baby."

"Yeah, little momma, you are. You've gotta tell Maverick."

"I don't know. I'd really rather wait and tell him in person. Do you have any idea how long they'll be gone?" she asked with concern.

"No more than you do. Cotton didn't really say much about it."

Her eyebrows furrowed as she asked, "So he didn't say anything to you about Sara?"

Feeling like she'd just punched me in the gut, I sighed and said, "No, and I didn't bring it up either. I figured if he wanted me to know he was leaving with his old girlfriend, he would've told me."

"That is so not cool, Cass. He basically claimed you as his old lady, and then doesn't have the decency to tell you what's up," she huffed.

"That's just it. He didn't officially claim me. We slept together and…"

Henley raised her hand, stopping me before I continued, and said, "It was more than that, and we both know it!"

"I guess it doesn't matter now anyway. He's halfway to Alaska by now, so I'll just have to wait and see if he comes back to me," I told her, trying not to let her see my heart was breaking at just the thought of him not coming back to me.

"Well, he'd be a damn fool not to come back to you. That Sara chick ain't got nothing on you, babe," she winked.

I ran my hand across the back of my neck, trying to ease some of the growing tension as I said, "She was his first love, and you've seen the pictures of her. She's beautiful and…"

"And so are you. You're all that and so much more!"

"It's not just that. They have *history*. You heard what Doc told Maverick. Cotton loved her, and it broke him when she left. She's the one that got away."

"She left, Cass. Never came to see him. Hell, she never even called the man. There's no coming back from that."

"I'm not so sure," I told her, fighting back the tears.

"Stop with the doubts, Cass. This isn't like you. You've always been sure of yourself. There's nothing for you to worry about with this chick. Besides, you're starting to sound like me, and that's never a good thing," she laughed.

I forced a smile and said, "Okay. I'll stop. Let's go call Dr. Roberts and see when we can get in to see her. I'll make an appointment too. It's almost time for me to get another prevention shot."

"So you'll go with me?" Henley asked excitedly.

"Of course, I'm going with you! I wouldn't miss it." I reached into Henley's purse and grabbed her phone. As I handed it to her, I said, "Now, give your man a call. It's time to tell him he's going to be a daddy."

"Are you sure? What if the test is wrong?"

"Call him, Lee Bug. He'd be pissed if you waited two weeks to tell him."

She nodded and pressed his number on her phone. Seconds later, her eyes lit up, letting me know he'd answered. "Yes, Maverick. I'm fine. I just needed talk to you about something. Have you got a minute?" There was a pause and then she said, "You know how I told you I thought I had the stomach bug? Well, it wasn't the stomach bug." She paused and smiled as she listened to him talk. "No… stop. I'm fine, Maverick. Just listen to me. When I wasn't feeling any better, I decided to take a pregnancy test. Well… it came back positive. I know it's early and we haven't talked about…" her voice trailed off as she waited for him to stop talking. "Yes, positive means pregnant," she laughed. I could hear his voice rumbling through the line, and even from across the room I could tell his was thrilled. "I'm about to call the doctor now. I'll know more after the appointment." Her smile grew wider and wider as she listened to him yammer on, and when he was finally done talking, she said, "I love you too. I'll let you know what the doctor says."

As soon as she got off the phone with Maverick, we called the doctor. They told her it would be a week before she could get her in for an OBGYN appointment, but the doctor sent her a prescription of prenatal vitamins to last until she got in to see her. In true Henley fashion, she spent the entire day on her computer, searching unique baby names and the latest designs for nurseries. While she was busy scoping out all the new trends, I spent the day working in the bar. My mind was in a complete blur the entire time I was doing inventory. I couldn't stop thinking about Cotton and wondering what was happening in Alaska. I wanted him home—safe and as far away from Sara as possible, and I felt like a selfish ass for feeling that way. I knew she was helping the club and should've been thankful, but I couldn't stop myself from wondering just how strong her connection with Cotton really was and what would happen to us if she decided to act on it.

Chapter 9

COTTON

AFTER A TWO-HOUR drive to Seattle, we boarded the plane without any delays. The flight actually left on time, and we were in the air just after nine. Stitch was sitting next to me, going over the files Big had given us on Derek. As our Enforcer, Stitch didn't like surprises and wanted to be sure we weren't missing anything. His eyes were glued to those damn papers until he was certain we were ready for what lay ahead. We were just about to land when he said, "I'm going to want to check all the artillery before we head out."

"Shouldn't be a problem," I assured him. Sara's security firm kept an overstock of weapons for emergencies, and Seth was confident we'd have everything we'd need. He guaranteed to have it waiting for us when we arrived at their firm. Stitch gave me a quick nod, then rested his head back on the headrest and closed his eyes, trying his best to prepare for the landing. Thankfully, it didn't take us long to get on the ground, and once we'd exited the plane, we headed straight for Sara's car. Once everyone was inside, Sara grabbed her phone and made a call to Seth.

"What's Derek's location," she asked. She waited for his answer and then asked, "Are you sure he's still there?" After another brief pause, she said, "Good. We're headed to the office now."

After she hung up the phone, she turned to me and said, "Seth has been monitoring Derek's GPS. He's been moving around a bit today, but right now, he is at the warehouse."

"And what about the other three?" Stitch asked.

"As far as he can tell, they aren't with him, but he's still trying to find their exact location in case we need it," she responded as she opened the glove box and pulled out her handgun.

As soon as Stitch spotted it, he took it from her hand, and even though she hadn't offered it to him, he gave her a quick chin lift and said, "Thanks."

Sara shook her head and smiled as she started the car. She put the car in reverse and pulled out of the parking lot. Thirty minutes later, we pulled into a parking garage next to a high-rise office building in the middle of Anchorage. When we walked through the main door, Sara was greeted by a security guard. After a brief conversation, he escorted her over to the main elevator. Once the doors opened, she motioned for us to follow.

When Stitch approached her, she said, "This shouldn't take long. Seth has everything you will need waiting for us in my office. You can check everything out before we go."

"You aren't going anywhere, Sara," I informed her. "You'll stay here until this thing is finished."

"But…" she mumbled as she crossed her arms.

"This isn't up for discussion. You need to stay here where I know you'll be safe."

"Fine," she mumbled.

"Gonna need the keys to your car," I smiled. Before she had a chance to argue, the elevator doors opened, revealing the hallway to her office. We followed her through the main doors. As usual, Stitch was right at my side, monitoring my every step. As we walked inside, I glanced around the room and wasn't surprised to see how contemporary it was. There was lots of gray and steel, giving the place a masculine feel. It was simple, but it suited her. Sara was never into all that girlie shit most women were into, and from the looks of her office, that part of her hadn't changed. As we continued to walk further into the room, my attention was drawn to a small photograph sitting on one of her bookshelves. I walked over to it and saw it was a picture taken when Sara and I were just kids, not long after she'd graduated high school. We were sitting on my bike outside the clubhouse, and I'm sure we were about to head out on one of our crazy adventures. Before we left, her mother stopped us to take a picture. I hadn't seen it in years. I couldn't help but notice the smile plastered on my face. It was a time long before Uncle Saul had died and I'd become President. It was a time when I was happy… really happy.

When I finally turned around, Maverick was standing there beside me. "We've got everything we need and more. Stitch has already checked them out, and they're locked and loaded," he explained as he handed me two of the handguns.

"Good. We need to check with Seth before we go. I want to know Derek's exact location before we leave," I explained.

"His office is just down the hall," Sara told me as she turned and walked out of the room. When we walked in, he was sitting at his computer and never even looked up until Sara spoke.

"Hey, Seth. Can you pull up Derek's GPS for me?" He looked up at her, and his face instantly softened when he caught sight of her. Anyone could see he had a thing for Sara, but she didn't seem to notice or care.

"Sure thing," he answered and quickly started typing on his computer. Seconds later, he said,

"He's left the warehouse. He's out on Dunbar Road. That's a new location. We haven't had a chance to have the team check it out. Maybe you should wait until he goes back to the warehouse."

"What's the full address?" I asked.

"22 South Dunbar Road," he answered.

I nodded then turned to Sara and said, "Need your car keys."

She placed them in the palm of my hand, and with Maverick and Stitch following close behind, I headed out to her car. It took us almost thirty minutes of driving through the outskirts of town to find Derek's location. Once we made it through a small, wooded area, we came up to an old, dilapidated house. The lot looked deserted; even the neighboring houses looked abandoned. When we got out of the car, we noticed there were locks on some of the windows, and the front door was also bolted from the outside. Hoping to find a way inside, I followed Maverick to the back of the house. Stitch went around in the other direction, making sure there were no surprises. The back door was closed, but it wasn't locked. As soon as we stepped inside the house, it was obvious the house was vacant. There was no heat, little to no furniture, and no sign of life anywhere in sight.

"Maverick, go check out the back room while I go out and check the shed," I ordered. "Stitch, see what you can come up with in the front rooms."

They both nodded and watched as I headed out the back door. There was an eerie silence as I walked toward the front door of the shed, sending an excited chill down my back. I reached into my back pocket for my gun and then pulled the door open. As I stepped in, it took my eyes a minute to adjust to the darkness, but once they had, I was sickened by what I saw. An entire wall was covered from floor to ceiling with pictures of Sara. My eyes slowly roamed over the large collage of photos as my mind tried to comprehend what I was seeing. Some of the pictures had been taken years ago, while others looked like they'd been taken just a few days ago. Each picture was more personal than the last. It was bad, but it got worse… much worse. I continued to walk further into the shed, and when I was just about to reach the back wall, all the breath rushed out of my lungs. It was Cassidy. Thousands of pictures of her were plastered all over the wall. Some of them had been taken as recently as last week. Panic surged through me as I stared at all the different photos of her, realizing for the first time he had been watching her for months and without any of us knowing; not only had he been stalking Sara again, he'd also become obsessed with Cass… my Cass. *Fuck*.

I shouldn't have hesitated. I should've left

right then and warned them it was worse than we'd thought, but I didn't. I was too caught up in the horror of what was in front of me to even move. When I finally stepped out of the shed, a blazing pain pierced through my lower back. The blast forced me to the ground, writhing in agony. I'd been shot before, but nothing could compare to the burning pain I was feeling at that moment. I could feel the life rushing from my veins as Derek dropped down beside me.

"I told you I'd have my revenge," he spat. The coward didn't even have the courage to face me. "You thought you could just take what was mine and get away with it?" Ensuring that the deed was done, he fired his gun again, shooting me for the second time as he said, "Wrong, *motherfucker*. Today, I take back what's mine... all of it."

I watched as a black SUV pulled up in front of the house. Derek rushed toward the passenger door and jumped in. He'd used a silencer on his gun, giving him just enough time to pull out of the lot before Stitch caught sight of them. Stitch raced toward the vehicle, firing off round after round as the truck started down the curvy road. I could hear the gunfire, but I had no idea what was happening. I tried to stay awake, needed to stay awake, so I'd know if he'd gotten Derek, but the darkness was consuming me, making it impossible for me to hold on. Just as I heard a thunderous explosion, everything went black.

Chapter 10

CASSIDY

SOMETHING WAS WRONG. I could feel it in my bones. I did what I could to push it to the back of my mind by busying myself in the bar, but every time one of the brothers walked through, it only confirmed my suspicions. Distress was written all over their faces, and none of them were talking, which worried me even more. I absolutely hated they wouldn't share what was going on, but it was nothing new—club business was never shared with the women. I just had to deal and move on. It was almost ten o'clock, and I hadn't heard anything from Cotton—no call, no text... nothing. If it weren't for the girls showing up at the bar tonight, I think I would've lost my damn mind.

"I've never seen Guardrail like this," Allie whispered. "It's freaking me out."

Remembering the look on his face when he charged through the bar earlier made my heart sink with the weight of my worry. I wanted desperately to ask him what was wrong, but I knew it was no use. I looked over at Allie and said, "Guardrail is great at what he does. Just give him some time to get it sorted."

"What exactly does he have to *sort?*" Henley snapped. "I just don't get it. Why won't he just tell us what's going on? It's obvious something's wrong."

"And it's not just him," Emerson piped in. "They are all acting like they're ready to blow."

"I can't take this. What if something happened to Maverick?" Henley spoke softly with tears filling her eyes.

"Stop. We aren't doing this. If we start the 'what if' game, it's just going to make things that much worse. The guys will be back in a day or so, and then we'll have a better idea of what's going on," I lectured.

"She's right," Allie said. "We've got to have a little faith here and trust that everything will work out."

Trying her best to change the subject, Allie turned to Emerson and asked, "When are you planning to head back to school?"

"I was planning to head back tonight, but ..." she trailed off. She took a drink of her soda, then said, "I'll probably just head back tomorrow."

"Let me know if you need any help getting

your stuff together. I know you're probably excited to get back to your old routines," I told her.

Her eyes dropped to the floor when she said, "No... not really. I like it here, and I'm not sure I want to go back."

"Then you should stay!" Wren smiled. "We'd love for you to stay..."

Before Wren could continue, Emerson shook her head as she said, "No... I can't. I know I have to go back and finish what I started. But it's going to be hard to leave everyone, especially Griff. I finally feel like I have my brother back, and I don't want to lose him."

"Honey, you're never going to lose him. Your brother thinks you hung the moon. There's nothing in this world he wouldn't do for you. Go finish up your classes, and if it feels right, come back when you are done," Wren explained.

"You guys really wouldn't mind if I came back?" she smiled.

"Are you kidding me? Heck, I'd love it. Then I'd have a chance to reclaim my Pac-Man championship title," Henley teased.

"Girl, you just don't give up, do you?" Emerson laughed.

"It's called determination," Henley responded proudly.

"I don't know about that," I snickered. "I'd say it's more like you're a sore loser. Always have been."

Henley turned to me with a horrified expression on her face and started spouting off all of her reasons why she wasn't a sore loser, making us all roar with laughter as we listened to her try to deny it. Thankfully, it was just the distraction we all needed to get us through the night. We spent the next hour talking, and I was starting to feel better about things, until the girls started leaving one by one. Allie and I were the only ones left in the bar when Guardrail came in to get her.

He walked over to her, and with a halfhearted smiled, asked, "Hey, All Star. You ready to call it a night?"

"Ready whenever you are," she answered. When he took a hold of her hand, she turned to me and whispered, "It's going to be fine. It has to be."

Just before they left the room, Guardrail spotted Clutch in the back of the bar. He stopped just long enough to shout, "Help Cass shut down the bar and do a final walkthrough."

"On it," he responded as he checked the back door and turned off the lights. I watched as he made his way toward the bar and quickly realized the man walking over to me wasn't the happy-go-lucky Clutch I adored—not in the least. The man coming toward me was full of rage as he cleared the empty bottles from the tables, causing them to clank roughly together in his arms when he walked. He stopped at the end of the counter and dropped them into the large metal trash can, glaring angrily as they all crashed at the bottom.

"Feel better now?" I asked sarcastically.

Without warning, he grabbed a full beer of bottle from the counter and threw it, shattering it against the back wall. I could feel the anger radiating off of him as he stood there, staring at the mess. "Fuck!" he roared. "I'm sorry, Cass... Just go on to bed. I'll clean it up."

"Might be a little difficult with that sling. I'll do it," I offered as I reached for the dustpan.

"Go, Cass. *Now*," he ordered. I could tell from his tone he wasn't in the mood to argue, so I handed him the broom and turned to leave.

Just before I walked out of the room, I turned to him and said, "You know, I was worried before, but seeing you like this... now, I'm terrified."

"Cass!" I heard him call out, but I was already halfway down the hall. There was no point in trying to talk to him. I knew he couldn't tell me what I wanted to know, so I ignored him and went to my room. I didn't even bother changing clothes before I crawled into my bed. I pulled the covers over me and tried to block out all worries racing through my head, but every time I closed my eyes, I was haunted by Cotton's face. I missed him. I missed him so much it hurt. I needed to feel close to him, so I threw the covers back and slipped down to his room. He'd told me he wanted me there, and it felt right as I lay down in his bed. I took a deep breath, letting his scent surround me, and I could almost imagine him there next to me, holding me, kissing me. Even though it was just in my mind, it was enough for me to escape my worries long enough for me to finally fall asleep.

I woke up early the next morning with Henley sitting at the foot of the bed. Her hair was falling loose around her face and it looked like she'd been crying. I sat up and said, "What's wrong?"

"Maverick still hasn't called. It's around seven, and I haven't heard anything from him. Something's happened to him, Cass," she cried.

I reached for her, pulling her into a hug as I said, "Oh, honey. It's still early... *really* early. I'm sure he's fine. Just give it some time."

"I kinda suck at this," she smiled. She wiped the tears from her eyes and said, "Old ladies are supposed to be able to handle this stuff. They're supposed to be tough... I'm not so tough."

"You're wrong about that, Henley. You're one of the strongest people I know. Stubborn as hell. You'll get through this just fine." I placed my hand on her shoulder and said, "Why don't we go to the kitchen and grab a bite to eat? I'm sure we'll hear something from them soon."

"Okay," she answered. "Can we make pan-cakes and bacon? I'm craving bacon."

"Bacon it is," I laughed. "Just give me a mi-nute to run to my room and change."

After I changed clothes, I found Henley in the kitchen, where she'd already started mixing the pancakes. We spent the next hour cooking enough breakfast to feed an army, and just when I was about to put everything on the table, Clutch walked in with Hoss, Cotton's youngest brother. Neither of them spoke as they filled their plates, and with the tension in the room bearing down on us, we all ate in silence. It was brutal, and when I couldn't stand it a moment longer, I got up and walked out the back door. Boozer was there, talking to Smokey, and didn't notice I'd come out. I tried to just ignore them, but when I heard Boozer say Cotton's name, I couldn't help but eavesdrop.

His voice was rattled and filled with concern as he explained, "He's pretty bad off. Guardrail said the doctors don't know if they can remove the bullet."

I felt like someone had stolen my last breath. I was completely stunned and couldn't make a coherent thought as I heard Smokey say, "He's the Prez, man. He's strong. Nothing's gonna keep him down. Not even a fucking bullet in the back."

"*Smokey*," I whispered as I fought back my tears. "What happened?"

"Shit, Cass," he answered, shaking his head with regret. "You weren't supposed to hear that."

"Well, I did. Is he still in Anchorage? Which hospital?" I asked. I had to get to him, one way or the other.

"I wish I could tell you, Cass, but you know I can't."

"Just nut up and tell me, Smokey!" I demanded. When he didn't immediately answer, I turned and headed back inside, slamming the door behind me. Guardrail was my only hope of finding out what was going on and where Cotton was. I found him working in Cotton's office.

He knew why I was there as soon as he spotted me in the doorway and said, "I don't know anything yet."

"Is he still in Anchorage?" I asked.

"Yes, at the county hospital," he answered. "But, Cass. He's sending Stitch home. Doesn't want anyone there but Maverick."

"But…" I started.

"Cass," he warned. "Just let it go. He wants you here."

I heard the words he was saying, but I wasn't listening. I'd already decided I was going to him, no matter what anyone said. "Okay," I answered. "Just please let me know if you hear anything."

"I will. And don't worry. He's going to be

okay," he tried to assure me, but I could hear the doubt in his voice, and it damn near broke my heart.

Chapter 11

COTTON

*I*T WAS LATE. *The bar was completely empty except for Cass and me. The party had finally fizzled out, and the only sound that could be heard was the low rumble of a song playing on the jukebox. Cass stood by the doorway, looking sexy as hell as she waited for me to come to her. Even from across the room, I could see that spark in her eyes shining brightly, making me want her even more. There was no better feeling than seeing that look and knowing it was just for me. I walked over to her, and when I lifted her into my arms, her legs instinctively wrapped around my waist.*

"You've been playing your tricks again tonight," I warned as I carried her down the hall.

Smiling innocently, she asked, "What tricks? I don't know what you're talking about." I kicked the door shut behind us and continued to carry her inside my room, only stopping when her back was pressed against the back wall.

"You know exactly what I'm talking about. You

know what this skirt does to me, woman. I can't take my eyes off of you whenever you wear it, and neither can anyone else," I growled.

"Oh, is that right?" she teased. Then she leaned closer, and just inches from my ear, she whispered, "Well… I may or may not be wearing panties under this favorite little skirt of yours."

"Fuck." Just the thought of her not wearing anything under that skirt made me come unglued. I immediately slipped my hands under her skirt and was relieved to find she was in fact wearing underwear. I looked up at her, only to find a devilish grin on her face.

"I said, may or may not… geez," she laughed.

"That's how you get yourself in trouble."

"Maybe that's the point," she grinned. "Maybe I like your punishments."

Having her wrapped around me had my cock throbbing against the zipper of my jeans. When I couldn't stand it a moment longer, I gave her lace panties a quick tug, ripping them free from her waist. I'd barely freed myself from my jeans when she tilted her hip, pushing herself down on my hard cock. She felt so fucking good, so tight, warm, and wet. I had to fight the urge to come right then and there. I put my hands on her hips, forcing her to remain still, so I could stop my dick from twitching for its release. She kept still for only a moment, but that was all I needed.

When I released my hands from her hips and planted them on the wall, she wound her arms around my neck and slowly began nipping at it. I eased back, then plunged *deep inside of her, giving her every inch of my dick, and relished in the sounds of her whimpers next to my ear. Her head fell back as she started to rock her hips against me, groaning in pleasure as she tried to inch herself up and down my cock. I withdrew again, only to drive into her over and over again, my pace quickening with every stroke. My rhythm became more and more demanding, and her nails raked across my back as tried to hold on. I should've slowed down, savored the moment, but my need for her was relentless and unforgiving. The moment her breath caught, silencing the little whimpers that always drove me wild, I knew she was getting close to the edge, which only made me want to fuck her even harder.*

"Cotton," she shouted as she clamped down on my cock, her orgasm pulsing against me. Fuck, she felt so damn good. I couldn't get enough of her. I could almost feel her tighten around me as her release jolted through her body.

Fuck. I wanted to stay lost in that memory of her coming undone, but I felt myself being pulled away. No matter how hard I tried to hold on, the warmth of her body was slowly disappearing, being replaced with the sounds of someone talking. When I opened my eyes, I saw Maverick standing at the end of the bed, talking to a doctor. Reality came rushing back, and so did the memories of being shot. I'd come back from surgery late last night, only to realize I'd lost some of the feeling in my lower legs, which made it difficult to move them. The nurse tried to explain how the doctors were unable to remove the bullet from my back, but got flustered when I grilled her for more information. The pain medication they'd given me made it difficult to stay awake, so I'd spent most of the night and morning completely out of it. I was finally coming out of the haze and tried to focus on what the doctor was saying to Maverick, but his voice was low, making it difficult to understand him.

"He's stable for now," the doctor told him. He coughed into his fisted hand and then continued, "Like the nurse said earlier, we managed to remove the bullet from his shoulder, but we were hesitant to do the same for the one in his back. During entry, the bullet grazed the lower cortex of his spine, and it has caused a great deal of swelling. It's lodged next to his spine, and the surgery to remove it is risky."

"Risky how?" Maverick asked.

"At this point, we don't know if the numbness in his legs is permanent. There is a very slight chance it will dissipate on its own. There is a greater chance it is permanent. In that case, the only hope would be to remove the bullet, which would be a difficult surgery. It could leave him permanently paralyzed, or it could solve the problem altogether. There is no way to be sure. We can leave the bullet where it is. With close monitoring and antibiotics, he should be fine, but without the surgery, he may not regain full use of his legs," the doctor clarified.

"I'll talk to him, but I already know what he'll say."

"It's important he understands. It's a gamble either way we go. Surgical decompression of the bullet from the spinal cord has been shown to improve neurological recovery, but there are no guarantees. We can't be certain the surgery will improve his chances of walking. There may be localized nerve damage, but we won't know until there's been further testing."

"What are his chances of walking without the surgery?" Maverick asked.

"Honestly, it doesn't look good."

I cleared my throat, drawing both of their attention towards me and said, "I want the surgery."

"You don't have to make that decision just yet. You've just come out of a pretty extensive surgery, Mr. Walker." the doctor answered.

"Doesn't matter. I want the surgery."

Maverick walked over to me and said, "You sure about this? You can survive if they just leave the bullet where it is."

"I don't want to just survive, Maverick," I snapped. "I've got nothing if I can't walk. You and I both know that."

Maverick nodded, then turned to the doctor and said, "He'll have the surgery. Make sure he has the best surgeon available. Don't care what it takes to get him here. Just make it happen."

With an apprehensive look on his face, the doctor said, "Well... Dr. Clayborn is the best. I'll have him schedule the surgery for three o'clock this afternoon. It should take six hours for him to complete. The nurses will be in later to prep you."

"I'll be ready," I told him.

As soon as the doctor walked out of the room, I turned to Maverick and asked, "What about Derek?"

"He's dead, Cotton. We heard the SUV start up, and Stitch raced outside to see what was going on. He saw them leaving and kept shooting until the truck ended up sideswiping a tree and flipped down a ravine. Before he could make it down the hill, the entire thing blew up in flames."

"So you're sure he's dead."

"The entire thing was up in flames, Cotton. No way he survived it. With you bleeding out, we didn't have time to wait for the fire to go out," he explained.

"Understood. And Delaney?"

"No sign of him. We think he was the one driving," Maverick answered. "So it looks like we got them both. Sara's team is looking into it, so we will know for sure soon."

I didn't like it, but for now, I had to believe

Derek had died in the explosion. It was the only thing I could do, so I said, "Just keep on top of it. Go back and check the vehicle, and let me know if you find anything suspicious."

"You know I will."

We talked off and on for hours while we waited for the nurses to come in to prep me for surgery. Even though Maverick tried his best to keep me distracted, it was hard to fight back the dark thoughts raging in the back of my mind. I knew it was bad—very bad—and the uncertainty caused a thousand 'what if' questions to bombard my thoughts. What if I couldn't ever walk again? Ride again? Fuck again? What if I was to be damned to a wheelchair for the rest of my life? What if I lost my presidency? What would that mean for me and the club? I just couldn't fathom any of it, and if there was any chance they could give me back my life with surgery, I was determined to try it, no matter the risk.

It was getting close to three o'clock when Maverick asked, "You sure about this?"

"Absolutely. No doubt in my mind," I assured him.

There was a light tap on the door, then Sara stuck her head inside the room and said, "I just wanted to come by and see you before surgery." She walked over to the bed and asked, "How are you doing?"

I could see she was worried, but I wasn't in

any place to reassure her or anyone else for that matter. I let out a deep breath and said, "I'm fine, Sara."

She brushed the hair from my eyes and said, "That wasn't very convincing, Cotton."

"I said I was *fine*," I snarled. She sighed with defeat as she walked out into the hall with Maverick.

I heard him tell her, "He'll be alright. He's just tired."

"I don't know," she said, just loud enough for me to hear. "I think he's in there feeling sorry for himself, thinking he may never walk again. And he's gotta stop thinking like that. He's got to get mad about this. He's got to get mad enough to fight, because he's going to have to fight with everything he has if he ever wants to walk again."

Maybe she was right, but that didn't change anything. I was still lying in a hospital bed with a bullet stuck in my fucking back, and until the surgery was over, I wouldn't know if I had anything to even fight for. Everything hung in the balance—every-fucking-thing. I tried to stop the doubts from consuming me, but it was damn near impossible.

Just like the doctor promised, the nurses came in at three to take me to surgery. In a matter of minutes, I was back in the operating room, fighting for my life. It was almost nine before I made it out of surgery. The doctors examined me time and time again and felt confident the surgery was a success, but I still had my doubts. Even after everything they'd done, I couldn't feel anything below my waist and was panicked I would never walk again. After spending an hour in the ICU, I was finally taken back to my room. I was still coming out of the fog of my anesthesia when I noticed Cassidy sitting quietly in the corner. She looked beautiful sitting there, staring at me. Her long, brown hair was cascading down her shoulders, and even though she was just wearing a pair of jeans and a sweater, I'd never seen her look so good. I wanted to reach for her, pull her close to me, so I could feel the warmth of her body next to mine. I wanted to feel that charge she gave me, get that lift I needed to set my mind at ease, but I knew I couldn't do it. It was like a double-edged sword—I had no idea if the surgery had worked, and I had to do whatever it took to protect her from the hell that lay ahead even if that meant hurting us both in the process.

"What are you doing here, Cass?" I growled.

She walked over to me and reached for my hand as she said, "I came as soon as I heard about the shooting. I wanted…"

"Weren't you told to stay at the clubhouse?" I snapped, hating to see the hurt that filled her eyes when she realized I wasn't happy to see her.

"Yes, but…" she mumbled.

"You were *told to stay put*, Cass. If I wanted you here, you'd know it." It killed me to say those words to her, but I knew it was the only way to protect her.

A dejected expression crossed her face as she whispered, "I'm sorry, Cotton. I just wanted to …"

"That's just it. This isn't about *you*, Cass. I'm the one who's been shot, and the last fucking thing I need to worry about is whether or not you are doing what you've been told," I roared.

With her voice strained as she was obviously trying to fight back her tears, she whispered, "I was worried about you and wanted to make sure you were okay."

"It doesn't matter. None of it matters. If you wanted to be an old lady… *my* old lady, then you should've done what you were *told*. Get back to the club, Cass," I ordered.

My heart sank deep in my chest, breaking right along with hers, as I watched it happen. Tears began to stream down her beautiful face, and seconds later, her light… that light that made my day complete, vanished, leaving her broken and cold. The very thing I'd tried so hard to protect was gone.

Her eyes dropped to the floor as she wiped the tears from her face and said, "I know you… I know you don't mean this, Cotton. I don't know why you're pushing me away, but I'll go… I'll do what you want." She looked up at me, her eyes pleading with me to tell her not to go, but I stayed silent. I couldn't take the chance. Tears filled her eyes once again as she said, "I gave you my heart, Cotton. I trusted you with it, and for some crazy reason I thought you would take care of it. But today, doing this... saying the things you said, you broke it. And I don't know if I'll ever be able to forgive you for that."

The woman who turned to leave wasn't the Cass I'd always known, and I wondered if she'd ever be the same again. As soon as she was gone, Sara stormed over to me and asked, "Why the hell did you just do that?"

"Had to," I answered.

"I don't understand you at all! That girl is obviously in love with you, Cotton, and there is no doubt in my mind you feel the same way about her, and you just broke her heart," she scolded.

"And how's she going to feel when I can't walk again, Sara? I know her. She won't walk away from me, even if it means I'll ruin her life. I couldn't live with myself, knowing I'd trapped her in that kind of life."

"You have to stop thinking the worst, Cotton. You're going to be fine," she tried to assure me.

"You don't know that. And until I know for sure, I'm not taking any chances. I won't let her give up her life for me. She deserves more than that."

"You don't get to make that decision for her, Cotton."

"I just did."

Chapter 12

CASSIDY

One Week later

"IT LOOKS LIKE you are about seven weeks pregnant," Dr. Westin told Henley. "We'll get a better idea of the actual date after your ultrasound."

"Seven weeks?" Henley asked nervously. "There was a night… it was a few weeks ago. We were celebrating, and I drank. A lot."

"It was early in the pregnancy, Henley. It's fine. Just refrain from all drinking for the rest of the pregnancy."

"Okay," she answered, sounding relieved.

"How is your morning sickness?"

"It's more like all day sickness," Henley pouted. "But it's manageable."

"Let me know if it doesn't get any better, and I will prescribe something to help. Be sure to take your prenatal vitamins every day, and I'll schedule your ultrasound for two weeks from today."

"Okay," Henley smiled.

Dr. Westin handed Henley a prescription for vitamins, and as she walked toward the door, she said, "Cassidy, I have the room set up next door for you. I'll let you go get ready while I check your blood work."

"Okay." I really didn't even see the point in getting the damn shot again. It wasn't like I was going to be sexually active anytime soon. But they did help regulate my cycle, and since I was already there, I decided I might as well do it. I followed Dr. Westin out into the hall, and she motioned for me to go into the room to my left. Once I was inside, I put on the scratchy paper gown and waited for the doctor to come in. It was the first time I'd left my room at the club, other than working at the bar, since I'd returned from Anchorage, and if it weren't for Henley, I'd still be there. The past week had been hard. I hadn't heard anything from Cotton since the day I left, and it was killing me. I had no idea how he was doing. My heart sank to the pit of my stomach whenever I thought about the possibility of him never walking again. I desperately wanted to see him, talk to him, and see for myself how he was really doing, but I didn't have that option. I kept hoping he'd change his mind and at least contact me. But he didn't, and I was beginning to think he never would.

When we finished up and headed out to the parking lot, we found Clutch and Smokey waiting for us. Just like always, Clutch was there, keeping an eye on us, but this time, he was too leery to ask either of us how it went. They followed us back to the clubhouse, but then left us, so they could go take care of some club business. I had no idea what was going on with the club, and I was getting worried. I was relieved when Guardrail finally called me into Cotton's office.

"He's doing better," he clipped.

"And?" I pushed.

"Cass, he's going to be there a while. Not sure how long it's going to take for him to get back home."

"I see... and he couldn't tell me this himself?" I snapped. I was beyond relieved he was going to be okay, but I couldn't imagine why he couldn't pick up the phone and just call me—let me hear it from him he was going to be okay. Besides, I didn't know what okay even meant. Would he be able to walk again? Would he be able to keep his presidency at the club? Everything was still up in the air, and I hated it. Cotton just kept dishing out the hurt, and I wasn't sure how much more I could take.

I could see it in his eyes—he knew I was right. He ran his hand through his hair and said, "Just thought you'd want to know, Cass. I know you've been worried."

"I understand… I might as well go on and tell you I've decided to move back to my apartment."

"*Okay*," he answered.

"Maybe you can get Tristan to cover my hours at the bar," I suggested.

"Why would I do that?" he questioned.

"I'm leaving, Guardrail. I really need some time to clear my head," I told him.

Without a moment's hesitation, he barked, "No. Not gonna happen."

"You can't make me stay here, Guardrail. I'm not officially claimed by Cotton, or anyone else for that matter. I'm just the bartender," I explained, my heart breaking as I said the words.

"You are more than just the fucking bartender, and you know it."

"Doesn't matter. I'm leaving. I've got to do what is best for me right now, and being at the clubhouse isn't it. I'll take some time off and eventually find a job somewhere else. It will be the best thing for all of us. Cotton doesn't need me distracting him while he's trying to get back on his feet."

He finally relented and even got Allie to help me find a secretarial job at a local pediatrician's office. The pay wasn't all that great, but if things went well, I would be promoted to a manager's position, which would mean a substantial increase in my salary. I gladly took the job, and in no time, I was easing into a real routine. It felt good to be back in my own apartment and away from all the memories of Cotton. I missed him. I thought being home would help, but every time I turned around, I found something that reminded me of him—an old t-shirt of his hanging in the closet, a song playing on the radio, or just a motorcycle passing by my window. He was everywhere. I couldn't get away from him, and I wasn't so sure I wanted to.

Thankfully, work helped keep me distracted. My first day went by in a complete blur. I was busy getting to know all the office routines and meeting all the doctors who worked there. They were all very nice, especially Sydney. She was in charge of billing and apparently knew all of the office gossip. I'd only been there a couple of hours when she came over, sat down next to me, and said, "Dr. Weston is getting a divorce."

"Which one is Dr. Weston?" I asked. I'd met them all, but I was still learning who was who.

"The older guy... with the weird hair and glasses. I heard his wife was cheating on him with her mechanic," she whispered. "And they had a prenup, so she won't get a dime."

"I hate to hear that... I mean, for Dr. Weston, not her."

"Girl, he's a complete jerk-face. Don't feel sorry for him," she huffed. "He's always got his adult diapers in a twist."

Laughing, I said, "Then I guess he got what was coming to him."

"You got that right." She paused for a minute then asked, "You like Italian? I'm in the mood for Italian. We should go grab some lunch together."

"Yeah, I'd like that."

"Cool beans. I know this great place I'll take you. They have killer pasta," she replied as she went to her desk to get her keys. Then she called out to the secretary out front, "I'm taking Cassidy to lunch. We'll be back in forty-five."

Sydney spent the entire lunch giving me the ins and outs of all the doctors and how things worked. When we got back, I didn't have much time to think about anything, much less Cotton. I spent the rest of the day sorting through the stacks of paperwork that had to be filed by the end of the day. When I finally managed to finish and headed home, I found Clutch waiting for me outside.

"Hey there, beautiful," he smiled. His back was propped against the brick wall of my complex, and he was wearing one of his baseball caps and a big smile. I'd noticed a few days ago he'd stopped wearing his sling and seemed to be fully recovered, and since he didn't need Smokey to drive him around, I'd seen a lot more of him. Especially after I'd left the club. He'd been by every day, so I wasn't surprised to see him standing at the front door of my apartment building.

"Don't you have anything better to do than harass me every day?" I teased.

"Nope," he replied as he followed me up to my apartment. As soon as I opened the door, he walked over and plopped down on my sofa. In a matter of seconds, he had the remote in his hand, surfing through all the sports channels.

"Well, make yourself comfortable," I laughed as I tossed my purse down on the table. "You know... you don't have to keep coming over here to check on me. I'm fine."

"Maybe so, but that doesn't mean I'm going to stop checkin'. I'm following orders after all," he smiled.

"Pfft. I doubt your prez even cares whether you check or not. Just stop wasting your time."

"Cass," he started. "I'd come, orders or not."

I walked back to my room and started changing my clothes. Through the closed door, Clutch shouted, "I just don't get it. So just because things didn't work out with you and the Prez, that doesn't mean you have to leave the damn club, Cass."

"I already told you. I needed some time to myself, knucklehead. Even you ought to be able to understand that."

"Well, I don't. There's no reason for you to give up everything just because ..." he started, but stopped when I walked back into the room.

"Just leave it. This is the right thing for me right now. I'm not saying it will be forever," I lied. I honestly had no intention of going back. Being around Cotton would just be too hard.

"You got anything to eat?" he asked as he got up and started walking toward the kitchen. "You haven't been around to cook, and I'm starving."

"So the truth comes out," I laughed. "You just miss me for my cooking."

"Now, you know that isn't true. I miss everything about you," he smiled, and I watched with surprise as a light blush covered his face. He quickly tried to recover by saying, "Well, not everything. You have that bad habit of bellowing out those weird songs. No one listens to that stuff, Cass. What's wrong with Adele or Demi Lovato?"

I gave him a light shove and said, "I can't believe you said that. I don't bellow... and it's not like I even know I'm doing it half the time, but I'll be sure not to sing around you anymore."

"*Whoa*... what's wrong with you?" he asked as he crossed his arms.

"What? Nothing's wrong."

"Oh, there is definitely something wrong, Cass. I've never known you to pout... ever."

I sighed and said, "And I'm not pouting now."

"Yeah, you are. You're pouting. No doubt about it."

"No... I'm not!" I snapped.

"Shit, Cass. What's going on? You're all on edge and moody... Ohhh, shit. I get it," he smiled.

"You get what, numb-nut?"

"It's that time of the month, huh? Feeling crabby and mad at the world? You want me to go get you some tampons or something?"

"Clutch!" I shouted. He took a step back and raised his hands up in defeat as I stepped toward him and said, "You are such an *asshole.*"

"Yeah, I can't help myself," he smirked. "But hey, let me make it up to you. What do you want for dinner? I'll go get whatever you want and one of those chick flicks you like so much."

I almost told him no, but I was lonesome and having him around helped take my mind off of things. "Yeah... I think that sounds good. Thanks."

"So what's it going to be? Chinese or Mexican?"

Just the thought of spicy food made my stomach turn, so I said, "Chinese. Definitely Chinese."

"You got it. You sure you don't need me to grab you some tampons while I'm out?" he laughed.

"You don't know when to stop, do you?" I laughed. "No. I'm good with Chinese and a movie."

It didn't take him long to return with a ton of Chinese food and more movies than we could ever begin to watch in one night, and it meant the world to me. We spent the night eating and watching movies, and he even helped me hang a few pictures in the hallway. He was just about to leave when he asked, "Whatcha got going on Friday?

"I don't know. Why?"

"I've been wanting to see that new movie, *Deadpool*. Wanna go?" he asked.

"Yeah. I think I can do the movie on Friday," I told him.

"*Cool*," he smiled. "I better get going. Be sure and lock up."

Even though it was almost midnight, I hated to see him go. "Okay. Thanks for the Chinese and the movies."

"Anytime," he answered as he closed the door behind him. With him gone, a lonely silence quickly filled my apartment. I tried to ignore it and headed for my room. I got into bed and tried to block out the sadness that kept trying to creep into my thoughts. There was no reason for me to feel sorry for myself. I had a good job, a roof over my head, and friends and family who cared about me. I had everything I really needed... except Cotton—the one thing I wanted more than anything else.

Chapter 13

COTTON

RECOVERY WAS A bitch. I spent the first few days after my surgery thinking it hadn't made a damn bit of difference, but the doctors were optimistic. I was becoming frustrated and wanted to tell the doctors to go to hell, but eventually, I started to regain more and more feeling in my lower legs. It was an odd sensation, like my legs had fallen asleep, but that feeling quickly turned into something more normal. Over the next twenty-four hours, the doctors saw my progress and were hopeful I would gain the full use of my legs again. After just a few short days, they had me up and on my feet. I had to use a fucking walker, but at least I was up. I worked my ass off, just trying to make it down the damn hall, but I didn't give up. I was determined to get my life back, no matter what it took. When I continued to get better, Dr. Clayborn decided it was time to move me over to a rehabilitation center across from the hospital. When I asked about doing my rehab at home, Clayborn was adamant I stayed close to the hospital. He wanted me there, so he could monitor my progress, at least until I got a bit stronger. Maverick and Sara both agreed with him, saying I would have fewer distractions if I stayed there while I completed my therapy.

I finally agreed with them, but I wasn't exactly happy about it. Dr. Clayborn promised me the rehab center was one of the best around, but I wasn't so sure. When I first walked in and saw all of the elderly people passing by, it felt more like a fucking nursing home than a rehabilitation center. I had my doubts about the place, but after being there for a couple of days, I knew I'd made the right decision to stay. I had my own room, and Sara brought me over a laptop and everything I would need to keep in touch with everyone at the club. As soon as it was set up, I sent an email to my mother and brothers, doing my best to assure them I was okay. In no time, I'd spoken to everyone—except the one person I actually wanted to talk to. As soon as I knew I might be able to walk again, I tried calling Cass, more times than I could count, but she wouldn't answer the damn phone. I even tried emailing her, but never got a response. She wasn't making it easy, not that I expected her to. She was shutting me out, and even though I knew I deserved it, that didn't mean I liked it. When Guardrail told me she was leaving the clubhouse, I wasn't exactly surprised. I knew I'd fucked up, but I would do whatever it took to fix it.

"Hey, there, Maverick. You mind if I steal him away for a little while?" Melody asked. She was one of the rehabilitation specialists who worked with spinal cord injuries. She was only five foot seven, but the girl was a total hard-ass. I was fairly certain she was trying to kill me during the first few days of therapy, but it was worth it when I managed to take a few steps without that fucking walker.

"Sure thing, Boss," Maverick laughed.

Melody turned to me and asked, "You ready for another go?"

"Always," I told her.

"We're going to the weight room today," she smiled.

"So, it's time for a little torture, huh?" I laughed. The weight room was always the hardest. She got a kick out of pushing me to my limit, but I didn't mind. I wanted to be pushed. The sooner I got my strength back, the sooner I could get back where I wanted to be.

"Thought we'd do some leg lifts and then hit the treadmill. Maybe hit the pool after that."

"Sounds good to me," I told her as I started toward her. Maverick gave me a quick chin lift as he watched me shuffle out of the door. Melody had stopped bringing the wheelchair after the second day, forcing me to walk everywhere we went, even if it took twice as long. I had to give her credit though. She was patient and made the time go by fast by talking nonstop the entire way. When we finally made it to the weight room, Melody headed straight to the vertical straight leg lift machine. I groaned when I noticed where she was going, knowing it was the hardest place to start. Most of the floor abdominal exercises only train one particular muscle, but leg raises on the pull-up bar work all your muscles at once. It was brutal.

"Alright, mister. Let's see what you got. I want two reps of fifteen to start," she smiled as she cocked her head to the side. I held back the profanities racing through my mind as I got into position and started my reps. When I'd started my second round, she said, "I'm going to turn on some music. Anything you want to hear?"

"I'm good with anything," I grumbled, thinking there wasn't a song in the world that could distract me from the burning pain in my gut, but I was wrong. After just a few beats of the loud, thumping music, a memory hit me with such a force it felt like the wind had been knocked out of me.

It was Doc's birthday, and the brothers had gone all out to show him a good time. Everyone brought food and presents, and he was genuinely touched by the gesture. Once the presents were opened and the food was eaten, the party really got started. Everyone was having a good time, especially Cass. It was one of the few times she'd actually managed to coerce Henley into coming to the clubhouse, and she was obviously pleased to have her there. Seeing how excited she was to have her sister around, I put Tristan behind the bar, giving Cass a chance to cut loose a little, and that's just what she did. She grabbed Henley and rushed out to the join the others on the dance floor, smiling and laughing as her hips swayed to the different rhythms that came blaring out of the jukebox. I couldn't take my eyes off of her. Every move she made had me completely captivated, and when she caught me staring, her lips curved into a knowing smile.

As soon as a familiar song began to rumble through the room, several of the girls became excited and rushed toward the dance floor. Cass gave them a welcoming smile as she continued to dance with Henley. I couldn't help myself—she had me spellbound. She'd blown into my life like a storm, weakening my guard and making me want more—much, much more. I sat there, drinking my beer at the bar, watching her as Maverick and Guardrail bitched back and forth over god knows what. Maybe I should've been listening, but there was only one thing that had my attention, and she was standing out on the dance floor. The two nosy asses both stopped talking when they noticed Cassidy walking in my direction.

She stopped a few inches from my knees and smiled as she tucked a loose strand of hair behind her ear. I was *tempted to pull her closer, but fought the urge. She finally placed her hand on my knee and leaned forward as she asked, "How 'bout a dance?"*

"Sorry, sweetheart. Not one to dance," I answered. Not liking the look of disappointment that crossed her face, I said, "Maybe some other time."

"Come on, Cotton. Dance with the girl," Guardrail teased, which only made the situation more awkward. I don't know what my problem was. I should've danced with her, but I was a fucking stubborn ass and refused to do it.

"Not happening," I snapped. I leaned back, resting my elbows on the bar, and smiled at her. "Trust me, Cass. You don't want to dance with me. I've got two left feet."

"Suit yourself, hot stuff. But just so you know, I'm not giving up. Sooner or later, I'll get you out on the dance floor," she smiled. "And dancing isn't the only thing I have planned for you."

"Is that right?"

"That's right. I've got my ways, Cotton, so consider yourself warned," she laughed. Fuck. I loved her laugh. There was nothing like it.

I leaned forward and reached for her waist, pulling her between my knees. Her breath caught when I brought my mouth close to her ear and whispered, "Looking forward to it."

Without skipping a beat, she said, "You and me both." With a wide smile, she walked back over to Henley and started dancing, completely carefree and happy.

"Hey… you okay?" Melody asked, pulling me from my memory.

I cleared my throat and said, "Yeah, I'm good. What's next?"

"How about a round on the treadmill?" she asked as she started toward the back of the gym.

I climbed on and waited for her to set the distance and rate. The machine quickly sprang to life, forcing me into action. The entire time I was walking on that damn thing, I was thinking about all the wasted moments. I couldn't stop berating myself for not dancing with Cass. I could've held her, felt her body next to mine, but I let that chance pass me by. Fuck. My mind was consumed with thoughts of her. I couldn't stop wondering where she was and what she was doing. I hated the thought, but I wondered if she'd been better off since she'd left the club. I knew she was okay, but I needed to be certain she was happy. Clutch had been keeping me posted, but it just wasn't the same. I needed to see for myself. I needed to know for myself if that light was back, even if it was just a glimmer. Realizing there was only one way for me to find out, I kicked up the speed on the treadmill and pushed myself even more. After an hour of walking, Melody led me to the pool. As soon as we were done there, she helped me back to my room. When I walked in, Maverick was talking on the phone.

"No," he growled. There was a brief pause and then with his voice raised in anger, he shouted, "I don't give a fuck what she said!" There was another pause and then Maverick roared, "If she leaves that fucking clubhouse, it's your head, brother. Find her and get her ass on the fucking phone." He hung up the phone and slammed it down on the table next to him. Fury radiated off of him as he glared down at it.

"You wanna tell me what the hell that was all about?" I asked.

"*Henley*," he grumbled.

"And?" I pushed, having no idea what the hell was going on.

"She's got it in her head that she wants to move back in with Cass until I get back home. She says she misses me and can't sleep."

Maverick had always been protective of Henley, but since the day she called to tell him she was pregnant, he'd taken it to a whole new level. He was on edge, worrying over every little thing, like all soon-to-be dads do. I knew he hated he wasn't there with her. He'd never admit it, but it was hard on him. We all knew he'd been through hell when he found out from the hospital that he wasn't John Warren's father, but Henley had given him a second chance. He was determined not to fuck it up, and I didn't blame him for being a little overprotective.

"I know you want her at the clubhouse. Hell, I want Cass there, but your girl's pregnant and needs her sleep, brother. Now that Derek's gone, there's no threat against the club."

"Maybe, but I can't keep an eye on her at Cass's place, and if something happens to her or the baby…" he growled.

I sat down on the edge of my bed, easing myself back against the pillows as I said, "If she goes to Cass's, we'll up the watch. Put two brothers on them around the clock. I'll get with Guardrail and have him send Clutch and Smokey over there to keep an eye on both of them. It won't be for much longer. We'll be home soon enough."

"We're not leaving here until you're ready."

"I'm ready now. Hell, I've been ready," I answered. "I'm giving them a few more days, but then I'm getting the hell out of here, brother. I'm tired of my life being on fucking hold."

"Just don't do anything you're going to regret later. Let them help you the best they can before you hightail it out of here," he laughed.

"I'll give it a few more days, but keep an eye on Melody. I'm pretty sure she's trying to kill me."

"She seems sweet," Maverick mocked.

"Nothing about that woman is sweet. Hell, she's the spawn of Satan," I groaned. "You have no idea."

"Sara called. Wanted to see how things were going and if you needed anything. She's planning to come by later tonight."

"I don't need anything," I answered. I was tempted to have him call her and tell her not to come, but I knew it wouldn't matter. If she was intent on doing something, she did it, damn the consequences.

It was after seven when Sara showed up with a basket full of food and drinks. After she sat it down on the table, she turned to me and asked, "Have you talked to her?"

"Who?" I asked, even though I knew exactly whom she was talking about.

"You know who. Has she answered yet?"

"Nope."

Her eyebrows furrowed as she asked, "So, what are you going to do about it?"

"Hell, if I know," I huffed. "I just need to get out of here so I can fucking see her."

"I know you're frustrated, but you'll be back to your old self soon enough. You just have to be patient," she said as she reached for her purse. "But don't worry too much about Cassidy. She loves you, Cotton. If you play your cards right, you'll get her back."

She gave my hand a light squeeze before she turned and left, giving me no chance to respond. I stared at the empty doorway for a moment, thinking of what I actually needed to do 'to play my cards right.' I grabbed my phone and made a call to Guardrail. It was time for me to make a statement with Cass, one she wouldn't be able to ignore, and I was going to need some help from my brothers to pull it off.

Chapter 14

CASSIDY

AFTER WORK, SYDNEY and I went to grab a bite for dinner, and by the time we were done, I was beyond exhausted. I felt like I hadn't slept in days, and my body ached everywhere— my head was pounding, and my neck had a terrible crick in it. Hell, even my butt hurt. I just wanted to take a hot bath and crawl into bed. Unfortunately, before I could go home, I had to make a run by the grocery store. It was the last thing I wanted to do after a long day, but I managed to get in and out of the store without much of a hassle. By the time I finally made it home, I was so tired I almost missed the large vase of roses sitting by my apartment door. The minute I saw them, I knew they were from him, which made my heart immediately start pounding against my chest. I quickly dropped my bags to the floor and reached for the card, eagerly opening it. My eyes scanned over it, again and again, until his words began to sink in.

Give me a chance to make this right.
Answer the phone.
Cotton

Unable to resist, I lifted the vase up to my nose and inhaled the delicate fragrance of the pink roses. And just like that, a little bit of hope snuck in, and I found myself smiling. I unlocked the door to my apartment, and as soon as it swung open, I was stunned by what I saw. Every inch of my apartment was covered with vases filled with roses, daisies, wildflowers, and lilies. Everywhere I looked, there was a different arrangement of flowers, each containing the same little white card nestled in the center. I rushed inside and grabbed several of the cards, impatiently opening each one to see what was written inside. Every card had the exact same message as the first. Damn. He was getting to me. As much as I tried to make myself believe I could forget about him and move on, deep down I've always known he had stolen my heart that first night we were together. I hadn't had many experiences with men, but I knew what we'd shared was something different... something I'd never get enough of.

The guys were in need of some wind therapy as they called it, and Cotton asked if I'd like to tag along. And of course, I jumped at the chance. I loved riding with him, feeling the vibration of the powerful engine beneath me as I snuggled up close to him. It was always fun, but there was something different about that day. There was a hungry look in Cotton's eyes when he looked at me, which only got more intense as the day progressed. When the rest of the brothers started back toward the clubhouse, he waved them off, taking me down a long, winding road nestled deep in the woods. He pulled up to an old, secluded cabin and cut off the engine. When I saw the Satan's Fury emblem on the front door, I knew we were at the club's hunting lodge, a place where none of the other women had ever been before. He stepped off the bike and extended his hand out to me. He didn't have to ask. He knew from the way I'd been holding him close, letting my hands wander a little more than usual, that I was feeling the same way. Without saying a word, I laid my hand in his and followed him up the steps.

Once we were inside, he released my hand and headed over to the fireplace. He glanced over to me and smiled as he started sorting through all the firewood stacked beside the hearth. While he got the fire ready, I stole a few glimpses around the large cabin. The rooms were simply decorated with just a bed and a TV—a perfect getaway for the guys at the club. When Cotton finally finished with the fire, the room quickly filled with a warm, incandescent glow. He took a step toward me with a look that made my breath instantly catch in my throat. I'd dreamed of being with him a thousand times and couldn't imagine wanting anything more. He brought his hands to my face,

gently cupping his palms along my jaw as he lowered his
lips to mine, kissing me with a passion I'd never even
known was possible. Our hunger for each other took over,
causing the kiss to become wild and heated. In a matter of
seconds, our clothes were tossed to the side, and Cotton
was lowering me to the floor. What started as rushed and
filled with carnal desire slowly slipped into something soft
and tender. I felt so safe in his arms, like nothing in the
world could harm me as long as he was holding me close.
We spent the entire night making love by that fireplace,
and neither of us could get enough of each other.

I brought my hand up to my neck, remembering the thrill I got whenever he kissed me there, and I didn't even notice when Henley walked up behind me.

"Holy moly. Your man definitely knows how to make a statement," she laughed. Her hair was pulled back in a ponytail, and she was wearing sweats with a t-shirt that said, 'How about... NO.' Without skipping a beat, she tossed her duffle bag on the sofa and asked, "What does the card say?"

I handed one to her and said, "He wants me to answer the phone when he calls. I've kind of been ignoring him."

"Why have you been ignoring him?"

"I don't know... maybe because he crushed my heart and soul when he kicked me out of his hospital room and told me I could never be his

Ol' Lady if I couldn't follow basic freaking orders. Remember any of that?" I sassed.

She rolled her eyes and asked, "So… you're saying you don't want to be with him anymore?"

"*No…* I didn't say that."

"Well, you'd be lying if you did. I know you're crazy over the man. He acted like an asshole, but can you blame him? He was about to have major surgery, and he was scared he might never walk again. He was freaking out, and he took it out on you."

"I know all of that," I mumbled. "He still didn't have to go about it like he did."

"No, but in his mind, he was probably thinking he was protecting you or something. You know how stupid men can be sometimes. You should just forget about what he said and call him," she smiled.

"Call him? *No…* I'll just wait for him to call me."

She grabbed my purse and started sifting through it until she found my phone. Once she'd found it, she handed it to me and said, "Suck it up, Buttercup. Time to call your man and get this thing sorted."

I took the phone from her hand and nervously pressed the button for Cotton's number. My stomach twisted into knots as I listened to it ring over and over again. After the fifth ring, a woman's voice came through the line, "Hello."

My heart sank. When I didn't respond, she spoke again, "Hello?... Cassidy? Are you there?" Even though I'd never heard her voice, I knew it was Sara, and just before I hung up the phone, I heard Cotton shout, "Sara, hand me the damn phone!"

I quickly hung up, and after I turned off my ringer, I slipped my phone into my back pocket. I looked over to Henley and said, "He didn't answer. I'm sure he's busy."

"Yeah, Maverick said he spends most of the day working with some spinal therapist. Apparently, they think she's trying to kill him," she laughed.

"I bet Cotton's loving that," I told her as I forced a smile, trying my best to disguise the fact I just wanted to crawl into my bed and hide. Luckily, she was too busy gawking at all the flowers to notice the tears that threatened to fill my eyes. Before she figured out I was about to cry, I turned toward my bedroom and said, "I'm gonna take a bath. Go put your stuff away and I'll be out in a little bit."

"Okay," she answered. Before I closed the door, she shouted, "I'll order us a couple of pizzas for dinner. We can catch up on our shows tonight."

Without answering, I shut my door and fell face first onto my bed, burying my head into one of my pillows. I tried to block out all the thoughts racing through my head, but it was impossible to stop thinking about Sara's voice on Cotton's phone. A part of me knew I was being irrational. Cotton had never given me any reason to be jealous where other women were concerned. From the beginning, he'd made no advances towards anyone, and even when the club girls would throw themselves at him, he'd turn them away. When I asked him about it, he'd laugh it off and say he only had eyes for me. But things were different with Sara. For whatever reason, he'd pushed me away and allowed *her* to stay there with him. I couldn't help but feel jealous about that. I'd always tried to be there for the people I cared about, doing whatever I could to help, but Cotton wouldn't let me do that for him. The day I went to the hospital, I had all intentions of supporting him, helping him... just being there for him, but he turned me away— basically banishing the very part of me that made me the person I am. He didn't want that from me, and that left me wondering what I was supposed to do.

It was pitch black in my room when I heard Henley shouting for me from the living room, "Pizza's here, hooker!"

I rolled over, quickly wiping the sleep from my eyes and said, "Coming!"

"I may have gone a little overboard with the pizzas. My eyes were bigger than my stomach," she yelled.

I opened my bedroom door, and when I found her standing in the kitchen, staring at four large pizza boxes, I said, "Yeah, you definitely went overboard, Lee Bug. There's no way we can eat all this," I laughed.

She shrugged her shoulders and said, "I wasn't thinking. Usually, the guys will finish up whatever I don't eat."

She made her plate and walked over to the couch, plopping down in my spot as she reached for the remote. Once she was settled, she said, "Dad's called a couple of times. He said he tried calling, but he hadn't been able to reach you."

"Yeah. I need to call him. I've just been busy with work and stuff," I explained.

"Just give him a quick call to let him know you're alright. You know how he worries," Henley fussed. We were both close to our father, and neither of us liked letting him down. He's never said the words, but I knew he worried about me working at the club.

"I will. First thing tomorrow," I assured her.

"Good," she said as she flipped through several channels, searching for our favorite show. "Hey, what happened to that picture of you and me that was beside my bed? You know... the one taken on the day Maverick gave me my property patch."

"No idea. Are you sure you didn't take it with

you?"

She shook her head as she took a big bite of pizza, and with her mouth full, she said, "Nope. Left it on the table."

I grabbed a couple of slices of cheese pizza and as I sat down beside her, I said, "I don't know. It'll show up."

"I hope so. I loved that picture of us," she told me as she reached for the remote. "So, what do you wanna watch?"

We continued to chat and gorge ourselves on pizza while we watched the latest episodes of *The Black List*. It felt good to have Henley back at home. Her smile and carefree demeanor made me feel like maybe everything would be okay. During the middle of the third episode, Henley fell asleep on the sofa. I covered her up with a blanket and turned off the TV before I went back to my room and went to bed. I woke up way too early in the morning to a loud banging on my front door. Reluctantly, I pulled myself out of bed and answered the door. I found Smokey standing on the other side, holding a box of donuts and smiling like the Cheshire cat. He was wearing a thick, black t-shirt with his Satan's Fury leather jacket and a pair of old beat-up jeans. Looking more like a rock star than a biker, he wore several leather bracelets on his wrists, and his long, jet black hair only enhanced those beautiful green eyes of his. Handsome or not, it was too damn early in the morning for me to put on a friendly smile.

"Smokey, it's six fifteen in the morning! What the hell are you doing here?" I groaned.

"Just checkin' on my girls. Cotton wanted an update," he smiled. "Brought you some warm donuts."

Of course, Cotton wanted an update. He wouldn't need a damn update if he hadn't been such an asshole. I let out a deep sigh as I opened the door and motioned for him to come inside. Once he sat the box on the counter, I said, "I've gotta get ready for work."

"Go on and do your thing. I'll make some coffee," he offered. "Is Henley still in bed?"

I looked over to the sofa, and when I noticed she was gone, I answered, "Yeah. She's been able to sleep a little later now that she's doing her last two classes online."

"Gotcha. No coffee for her."

"Nope. It's not good for the baby anyway," I explained.

He nodded and said, "Oh, yeah. I didn't think about that."

"I'll be back in a minute," I told him as I walked into my room. After I was showered and dressed, I went back out to check on Smokey and found him sound asleep on the sofa. I decided not to wake him and left for work. When I got down to my car, I reached for my keys so I could open the door, but before I found them, I noticed the door was already unlocked. It wasn't like me to not lock my door, so I stood there, staring at the unlocked door as I tried to think back through my steps from the night before. I couldn't even remember parking my car, much less locking the dumb doors. It was just another crazy thing I'd done since I'd come back from Anchorage. I eased the driver's side door open and peered cautiously inside, but didn't find anything that looked suspicious. After thinking about it for a second, I convinced myself I'd been distracted and just hadn't locked it. I'd had a lot on my mind over the past couple of weeks, and I'd just forgotten to do it. Doing my best to shake off my nerves, I got in the car and headed to work. The entire way there, I berated myself for being such a damn mess. I needed to pull it together. I was tired of spending all of my time trudging through the swamps, worrying over Cotton. It was time for me to think about myself and try to find a way to make myself happy, even if that meant finding a way to move on without him.

Chapter 15

COTTON

S HE WAS JUST trying to help, but ended up fucking everything up.

Sara had come by to check in. We'd been talking for several minutes when Dr. Clayborn came in. We were discussing my status, and just as he was about to leave, my phone started ringing. I nodded over to Sara, letting her know to take care of it. But instead of silencing the call, she answered it.

"Hello?" Then she paused for a few seconds. A strange expression crossed her face as she lowered the phone and looked down at my screen. When she read the name displayed, she quickly brought it back to her ear and asked, "Cassidy? Are you there?"

The second I heard Cassidy's name, I shouted, "Sara, hand me the damn phone!" But by the time she put the phone in my hand, Cass was no longer on the other end. I immediately tried to call her back, but she didn't answer. I dragged my hand through my hair and groaned, "Fuck."

"I'm sorry," Sara told me. "I was just trying to help."

"No telling what she's thinking now."

"She wouldn't be thinking anything if you'd just been straight with her from the beginning," Sara snapped.

"You know why I did what I did," I barked.

"Doesn't mean it was right. Cass had a right to make up her own mind, but you didn't trust her enough to let her do that." She stepped closer and said, "You took that away from her. It was selfish, and it isn't the way love works, Cotton. You have to respect her feelings. They are just as important as your own."

"I was protecting her!" I shouted.

"Keep telling yourself that, Cotton," she said sarcastically and then walked out, letting the door slam behind her. I knew there was some truth to what Sara had said. I thought I'd sent Cass away to protect her, but I never took the time to consider how my actions would affect her. She'd always been a nurturer, always taking care of the people she loved, and it was one of the things I loved most about her. The more I thought about it, the more I realized how badly I'd fucked up. I was more determined than ever to talk to Cass. I'd been trying to call her for two days, but she wouldn't pick up the damn phone. I was becoming more and more frustrated by the minute, and I was taking it out on everyone around me. Hell, the nurses had all but stopped coming into my room, and Maverick was doing what he could to keep

his distance. I couldn't blame him. Hell, I didn't even want to be around me. It would've been better if I could just talk to her. I just needed to hear her voice, to know I hadn't lost her by sending her away. I missed her—all of her—and as I sat there alone in that room, thinking of all the things I loved about her, I knew I'd do anything to fix things between us. The only thing that was keeping me going was knowing that the doctors were going to let me go home in a few days, so I wouldn't have to wait much longer to lay my eyes on her. I just had a few more sessions with Melody, and then I'd be on my way.

When I came in from my workout, I had a ton of emails to sort through. My brothers and mother wanted to hear about my progress, and Guardrail wanted to give me an update on things at the club. He and the brothers had been busy preparing for our Charity Run for children with Down's syndrome, and he wanted to go over the final details with me. It was just a few weeks away, and I wanted to be there—it was something that meant a lot to me. It wouldn't be our first charity run, but it held special meaning for us all. When our brother, Skidrow, was killed a few months back, his wife, Dallas, had a hard time getting back on her feet. Her youngest, Dusty, was diagnosed with Down's before he was even born. Skid had always been there to make sure his son had whatever he needed, and after he died, the club decided to start an annual fundraiser to help families in our area that had children with special needs. We were expecting a large crowd, so hopefully, we'd be able to raise a good deal of money for some pretty awesome kids.

I'd just responded to his email when Maverick walked in with a handful of sandwiches and drinks. Until I saw him, I hadn't even realized I hadn't eaten. He set the bag of food down beside me and said, "Figured you might want something to eat."

"Yeah, food would be good."

"How did things go with Melody today?" he chuckled.

I shook my head and said, "That girl is going to be the death of me for sure, but I can't complain. Haven't had to use that damn walker in a couple of days."

"Give it a couple more days, and the cane will be gone, too."

"That's the plan," I told him as I reached for my sandwich. "Guardrail messaged me. Things are all set for the Charity Run."

"Yeah, he's been busting his ass trying to get everything sorted."

"Need to be there," I grumbled.

"We'll be there soon enough."

I tossed the bag of food back onto the table

and said, "I need to get the hell out of here for a little while. The walls are closing in on me."

"Can't blame you there. Hell, I feel like I've aged twenty years just sitting in this place over the past few weeks," he laughed.

"You and me both, brother. I don't care where we go. Let's just get the fuck out of here for a few hours."

"You got it. I'll let them know we're heading out. I'll meet you out front," he told me as he headed toward the door.

We spent a few hours driving around Chugach State Park. While it was a beautiful place, I couldn't stop thinking about how much I'd rather be at home. I missed my drives along Cape Flattery. I missed the club and my brothers. I missed Cass. When it started to get dark, we headed back to the center. As soon as we got back to the room, Maverick headed out front to call Henley. She'd had a doctor's appointment earlier, and he still hadn't heard from her. The room was too damn quiet, and I needed to blow off some steam, so I headed to the gym for an extra workout. I couldn't get Cass out of my head. I needed to see her, so I could see for myself she was really okay. I felt better knowing the brothers were keeping an eye on her, but it wasn't the same. It was time to talk to Dr. Clayborn. As soon as I got back to my room, I called his direct line and left him a message, letting him know I wanted to see him as soon as possible. Thankfully, I didn't have to wait long for him to show up at my door.

"I just finished my rounds and thought I'd stop by on my way home," he told me as he entered the room.

"I appreciate that," I told him. "Wanted to tell you I'm heading home."

"You've done well, Mr. Walker. I don't have a problem with you taking that next step as long as you can assure me you will keep up with your rehab. I'll put in some calls and get you lined up with a specialist in your area for further check-ups. A few more weeks of hard work, and you'll get rid of that cane."

"I'll do whatever it takes," I promised.

"I'll get your release papers ready first thing in the morning."

"Thanks. I appreciate all you've done, doc."

He smiled and said, "Glad I could help. It's good to see you back on your feet."

He shook my hand and headed for the door. I finally felt a sense of relief. I was going home, and once I got there, things were going to change—drastically. I'd made my mistakes, but I wasn't going to let them destroy what I had with Cass. Come hell or high water, she would be mine again.

Chapter 16

CASSIDY

BY THE TIME I'd gotten home from work, Henley was already gone. She'd promised Dallas she'd look after Dusty for the night, which meant I'd have the apartment to myself if I could just find a way to get rid of Smokey. I'd spotted him following me home from work, so I knew he'd be knocking on my door at any minute. Biding my time, I went to the fridge to grab the pitcher of sweet tea I'd made the night before and was surprised to see it was already gone. Henley didn't care for sweet tea, so unless her pregnancy completely changed her taste buds, I knew it wasn't her. That meant Smokey or Clutch had been helping themselves to the contents of my refrigerator again. Assholes. Trying to ignore the empty pitcher of tea that sat in my fridge, I grabbed a bottle of water and headed over to the thermostat. I was freezing, had been all day, and it was only getting worse. I just wanted to lie down for a minute and warm up, so I walked into the living room and set my bottle of water on the coffee table. I reached for the remote before curling up on the sofa with my favorite blanket wrapped around me. I was instantly hit with the strong scent of a man's cologne. I brought my blanket up to my nose, and sure enough, it smelled like Old Spice and cigarettes. Damn. I couldn't get away from them. I was just about to get worked up into a real tizzy when there was a knock at the door.

I threw my blanket back and headed for the door. When I opened it, I wasn't surprised to see Smokey standing there. Before he even had a chance to speak, I stepped forward and poked my finger at his chest as I scolded, "When you drink a gallon of milk or a pitcher of tea, don't put the empty carton back in the stupid refrigerator."

"Okay," he said apprehensively.

I turned and headed back into my apartment. When I heard the door close behind me, I asked, "Are you hungry? We have some leftover pizza in the fridge."

"Nah, I'm good. I've gotta head over to Mom's in a bit to check on her furnace. I'll grab something there," he explained.

I smiled and said, "Can't blame you there. Your mom is an amazing cook. I'd wait all day for a piece of her lasagna."

"You want to tag along?" he offered. "She'd love to see you."

"Thanks, but I can't tonight. I have to get some laundry done or I won't have anything to wear to work tomorrow."

"Not sure I see that as a problem," Smokey teased. "But I'll come back later to help you bring it back upstairs."

"That would be great. Thanks, Smokey."

"Not a problem, doll," he answered as he turned toward the door. "Clutch will be by in a bit. He had to run by the clubhouse to see Guardrail about something first."

Needing some time to myself, I said, "Tell him I'm fine. There's no need for him to come."

Walking toward the door, he laughed as he said, "I'll tell him, not that it's gonna matter."

I locked the door behind him and returned to my spot on the sofa. I started flipping through the channels, searching for something that might be boring enough to let me fall asleep for a little while. I stopped when I came across some old western with John Wayne. Just seeing it reminded me of Cotton. He'd always had a thing for old westerns, saying it was something he loved watching with his dad. It was crazy how some old movie could make me miss him so much. I remembered I'd received several text messages and emails from him over the past few weeks, but I hadn't read them. I just didn't have the strength to even look, so I just left them in my inbox. I grabbed my phone and stared at the screen for several minutes before I had the nerve to open one of the text messages. The first few messages were typical, bossy Cotton:

Monday, (two weeks ago)
Cotton:
Answer the phone, Cass.

Wednesday, (two weeks ago)
Cotton:
This is crazy. I shouldn't have sent you away. I've said that. Over and Over. I don't know how many times you need me to say it.

There were tons of these short, berating messages, and when I got tired of trying to sort through them, I opened my email. There were over forty messages waiting to be read, but one instantly caught my eye. It was labeled *Lonestar*, the title of one of my favorite songs by Norah Jones, and he'd just sent it a couple of days ago. I quickly opened it and began to cry as I saw what was written inside.

Cass,
I was sitting here, listening to one of the songs you used to sing. I've always liked them, especially when you were singing them. But tonight, this one got to me. It re-

minded me of you. Every time I close my eyes, I see your face that day in the hospital. I watch the spark in your eyes disappear over and over again in my mind. Knowing that I was the one who stole that light from you has haunted me since the day you walked out that door. There's nothing I wouldn't do to bring that light back, and I will never stop fighting for the chance to make things right. It's made me realize something… Cass, you are my Lonestar.

Always,
Cotton

By the time I'd finished reading the letter, I was crying uncontrollably. Cotton had let his guard down, and for the first time, I saw a vulnerable side to him… a side I wanted to treasure and hold close to my heart. I read through several of the emails, finally learning about his rehab facility and all the work he'd been doing so he could walk on his own again. I couldn't help but laugh when he went on and on about some lady he called his own personal drill sergeant. Some of the letters were more like journal entries, just short messages telling me about his day, while others were some of the most endearing letters I'd ever read. Once I'd gone through all of the emails, I went back to my text messages. I quickly skimmed over the first six or seven messages, until his words stopped being so demanding and intense. As I'd hoped, they eventually turned into something completely different. I needed to know he was capable of that kind of honesty. Reading his words changed things. My heart was softening after all the hurt and humiliation of being sent away. Until the letters, Cotton had shown no understanding of my feelings. Now, maybe there was a chance. I couldn't stop the tears from streaming down my face as I read the words written in all the different messages. I was so torn. I loved him so, but I wasn't sure I could ever really trust him with my heart again.

Sunday, (a week ago)
Cotton:

I'd rather be in hell than in this place. I know I shouldn't complain. I'm doing better. The walker is gone and replaced with a cane. It's progress, but it's not enough. I want to be home.

Cass, I'm sorry. I miss you more with each breath I take.

Friday, (less than a week ago)
Cotton:

Remember the day you told me about your grandmother's house, and how it was your favorite place? I wish I were sitting on that swing with you right now, looking out at the ocean. I wish I were anywhere with you.

Sunday, (this week)
Cotton:
I miss your face, your smile, and the way
your eyes light up when you get your way. I
miss the sound of your voice when you sing.
I miss holding you in my arms, kissing you,
making love to you. You'll always be mine,
Cass. I'm not giving up on you.

I'd read through so many messages, each one
tugging at my heart, but one… one short text
message took my breath away.

(Two hours ago)
Cotton:
I'm coming home.

I was still trying to wrap my head around
everything I'd just read when someone knocked
on my door. I wiped the tears from my face,
grudgingly threw the covers back, and got up to
answer the door. When I opened it, Clutch was
standing there with a big smile on his face, holding a bag of groceries. He was wearing an old
baseball cap and a pair of faded jeans with his
favorite Braves t-shirt. As he stepped inside, I
noticed he hadn't shaved in several days, making
me wonder if he'd decided to grow a beard, but
before I could say anything about it, he asked,
"Hey, beautiful. You okay?"

"I'm fine. It's just my allergies acting up," I

lied as I tried to rub the remaining tears from my eyes. I could've told Clutch about the letters, but they were written for me, just me, and I didn't want to share them with anyone.

He gave me an apprehensive look, but didn't question me about it. As he walked into the kitchen, he asked, "You hungry?"

"Yeah, I could eat something. Whatcha got?"

He started unloading all the groceries on the counter and said, "Thought I'd make us a pot of chili."

"With one of your grilled cheese sandwiches?" I asked excitedly. His grilled cheese sandwiches were legendary.

"Of course," he smiled. "I know how you like them."

I looked over to him and said, "You know, you don't have to babysit me, Clutch. I'm fine. Besides, I'm sure all your little girlfriends are wondering where you've been lately."

"Nah... they know I'm worth the wait, darlin'," he snickered.

"*Whatever*," I teased. "You are so full of it."

"Maybe so, but I haven't heard any complaints," he laughed as he put the burger meat in the skillet. In no time, he had everything simmering on the stove. We made our plates and brought them into the living room to eat. Once I was settled on the sofa, I looked over to Clutch, seeing he'd already kicked back the recliner and made himself comfortable.

I tossed the remote over to him and said, "Find something."

"You're giving me free reign with the remote?" he teased. "I feel special."

"Don't get used to it," I warned. "It's just my way of thanking you for dinner."

He smiled as he started going through all the different channels, and I wasn't surprised when he stopped at the movie, *Silver Linings Playbook*. I knew he didn't care for watching that movie, but he remembered it was one of my favorites. He was always thoughtful of things like that. It was one of the things I liked most about him, that and his goofy personality. He always knew how to make me smile. We ate our dinner, only talking between commercials as we watched Bradley Cooper do his best to keep up with Jennifer Lawrence. It was the perfect distraction. My stomach was full, the movie was just as awesome as I remembered, and having Clutch around was just what I needed to keep my mind off Cotton. He only made it halfway through the movie before he was sound asleep in the recliner. His muffled snore sounded like an old, dying hound dog, but I didn't mind. Despite my earlier disposition, I actually enjoyed having his company.

When the movie was over, I was tempted to grab my phone and read through all of Cotton's emails again, but figured it would just make me miss him even more. I decided to wait up for Henley, so I reached for the remote and started looking for something to watch until she got home. I'd been scrolling through the channels for several minutes when I got an eerie feeling something or someone else was in the room with me. Thinking it might be a mouse, I muted the TV and tried to see if I heard anything moving around in the apartment. I didn't hear anything, but still felt a gnawing sensation I wasn't alone. I sat up straight on the sofa and looked around the apartment, searching all the dark corners of the room, but I didn't see anything. I was just about to give up my search and lie back down in my spot when something in the window caught my eye. I turned back to get a better look at the fire escape, and a rush of adrenaline surged through me when I realized there was a man standing there, looking at me through the glass. It was dark, but I could still see his eyes were glaring directly at me. There was something about the way he was looking at me that gave me the feeling I'd seen him somewhere before, but the pure terror I was feeling made it impossible to recall the memory. And crazy enough, he knew I'd spotted him, but he just stood there, rooted to his spot as he stared back at me. His eyes were hollow and cold, making me feel a fear I'd never felt before. I wanted to run, to shout out for him to leave, but I couldn't do anything except stare right back at him.

After several seconds, I finally forced myself off the sofa and immediately started backing away from the window as I yelled, "Clutch! Wake the hell up!"

The figure didn't move, but my scream quickly got Clutch's attention. He shot to his feet and barked, "What is it? What's wrong?"

I pointed toward the window and shrieked, "Someone's out there!" I'd only looked away for a second, but the man was already gone.

"Call Guardrail," Clutch ordered as he raced over to the window, quickly releasing the lock before he raised it. Before he stepped out on the ledge, he drew his gun and said, "Lock this behind me and stay put till they get here. *I mean it*, Cass. Don't open that door unless it's one of the brothers!"

I nodded and watched as Clutch disappeared into the darkness. I heard his boots stomp up the metal steps as he went after the stranger. When I couldn't hear him any longer, I called Guardrail's number, and by the time he answered, I was a complete and total wreck. My voice crackled with nerves as I said, "Someone's here, Guardrail. A man is outside on my fire escape, and Clutch just went after him!"

"Stay where you are. We are on our way. Lock your doors and windows. Don't let anyone in until we get there," he ordered.

"Okay," I answered, but the line was already dead. Seconds later, my phone started ringing. When I looked down, Smokey's name was flashing on the screen. I quickly answered, "Hello?"

With his voice sounding a little panicked, he asked, "Hey, doll. You okay?"

"Yeah, Smokey. I'm fine... but Clutch just went after this guy and ...," I started.

"Don't you go worrying about Clutch. He'll be alright. You just try to relax.... I'm close. I'll be there in two minutes. Just hold tight until I get there."

I tried to hold back my tears as I asked, "Smokey?"

"Yeah?"

"Can you stay on the phone with me until you get here?" I pleaded. I knew it was silly, but just hearing his voice was settling my nerves.

"Yeah, I can do that," he answered. I was just about to go sit on the sofa when I heard two gunshots fired off in the apartment above me. Seconds later, there was a loud thud that echoed against the ceiling.

"Shit," I screeched. My heart started pounding wildly against my chest as I said, "Smokey... gunshots. Two of them in the apartment above me."

"Did you lock all the windows and doors?" he asked.

I stared at the window, too scared to move

from the spot where I was standing, and said, "No."

"Cass, I know you're scared, but you gotta go lock that window, doll," he ordered.

Knowing he was right, I forced myself to move forward, and despite my trembling hands, I managed to secure the lock. Once it was done, I told him, "Okay. I did it."

"That a girl. You did good, Cass. I'm about to pull in. You doing okay?"

"No, Smokey. I'm not. I hate myself for it, but I'm freaking out. I'm worried about Clutch. What if someone shot him?" I cried.

"Don't. Clutch will be fine," he assured me.

My heart started to race when I heard the sound of footsteps walking across the floor above me. My heart was racing as I said, "I'm scared, Smokey. What do you think is going on upstairs?"

I heard his keys jingle as he turned off his truck. He closed his door before he said, "I have no fucking idea, but we're about to find out. The boys will be here any minute. I'm on my way up. Stay on the phone, and I'll tell you when I get there."

"Okay," I answered. A few moments later, I heard someone pounding on my door. "Smokey, is that you?"

"It's me. Open up." I quickly released the deadbolt and opened the door. The second I saw him, I rushed over to him and wrapped my arms around his neck, hugging him tightly.

I was still holding on to him when I heard a commotion upstairs. I immediately released my hold on him and said, "You've got to go see about him. Please."

From the look on his face, it was clear he was struggling with what he should do. "I'm not leaving you alone."

There was more ruckus above us, making me plead with him even more. "Smokey, if he's in trouble…"

He finally agreed and said, "You don't leave this apartment. I'll be back as soon as I can."

"Okay," I promised.

He reached in his back pocket for his second handgun and gave it to me. "Just in case."

I nodded, and as soon as he walked out of the apartment, I shut the door and locked it behind him. Feeling a nervous wreck, I paced back and forth in the kitchen, trying my best to hear what was going on in the apartment above me. It felt like an eternity, but it'd only been a few minutes when I heard a knock at my door. "It's me, Cass."

I rushed over to unlock the door, and when I opened it, I found Clutch standing there. When I noticed his blood-soaked shirt, I almost lost it.

"Don't look at me like that, Cass. I'm fine," he assured me.

"There's so much blood," I cried.

"It's not mine. Go grab your stuff. We're going to the clubhouse," he ordered. His tone was forceful, which only made me worry more. It wasn't like him to be so short with me.

"I'm scared, Clutch. Are you going to tell me what's going on?"

"Everything is going to be fine, but we need to get going… *now*, Cass. Grab your stuff, and I'll send one of the prospects to get Henley's stuff later."

"Henley… she's babysitting Dusty. I need to tell her not to come back here."

"I know, Cass. It's already been taken care of. Now, put a move on it. We've got to get the hell out of here."

"Okay," I answered as I rushed to my room and threw a few things in a duffel bag. My mind was in a complete blur as I grabbed my purse and headed for the door. I had so many questions swirling around in my head, but I knew better than to ask. I knew something had happened with the guy from my window—that much was obvious from the blood on Clutch's shirt, but I had no idea what. I desperately wanted Cotton. No matter what was going on, he'd always managed to make me feel safe, but since he wasn't around, I had to figure it out without him. I had to. Falling apart in the middle of all the chaos wouldn't help anyone.

As soon as we got back to the clubhouse, Clutch said, "I'll get you to your room."

He took my hand and started leading me down the hall. We were almost to my room when I asked, "But what about you. Where are you going?"

"I've got some things to take care of, Cass."

I reached for his arm and said, "You have to tell me, Clutch. I need to know. That man... has he been in my apartment? Was he the one moving my stuff around and eating my food? Was it his cologne I smelled on my blanket?"

"There's no use in thinking about all that now, Cass. It's late. Try to get some sleep," he told me before he freaking left.

I lay down on my bed and tried to settle my nerves, but there was no freaking way in hell I was going to be able to sleep. I couldn't stop thinking about that stranger being in my apartment, going through my things. The fear was suffocating, and after a few hours of staring at the ceiling, I finally gave up and went into the entertainment room. I curled up on the sofa and turned on the news, praying the boring, monotone sound of their voices might help settle my nerves. Unfortunately, it didn't. I was still up several hours later when Clutch walked in, looking as tired as I felt. He'd taken a shower and changed his clothes, but the image of his blood-soaked shirt was still burned into my memory. I almost cried as I watched him walk over to me, but the moment he sat down next to me, I immediately started to feel better. He'd always been such a good friend, and it meant so much to me he was looking out for me. Without saying a word, he put his arm around my shoulder, and once I laid my head on his shoulder, I finally managed to fall asleep.

Chapter 17

COTTON

I'D GONE TO bed with one thing on my mind—Cass. When I sent her away, I was being selfish. I was used to being strong and in command, and I didn't want her to see me any other way. I knew I was hurting her, but it was what I wanted and it never occurred to me she had a say. Looking back, I understood how wrong it was. I finally understood that loving someone was about respecting the feelings of the person you love. It took getting my body blown to shreds to get it through my thick damn head. I wasn't sure if she would ever forgive me. If the roles had been reversed, I wasn't sure I'd be able forgive her, but I had to try. I had to get home and do whatever it took to make things right with her. I'd just need time to make her understand... to explain all my reasons for pushing her away, and to find a way to make her forgive me for being such a damn fool. I just needed a chance, and then I could spend the rest of my life making it up to her. That chance was almost ripped away from me when Derek showed up on her fire escape. When Clutch went after him, he discovered Derek had been hiding out in the apartment above Cass. None of us were sure how long he'd been there, but he'd managed to gather quite a collection of her things. And just like before, there were pictures… everywhere. I could only assume he hadn't made a real attempt to hurt her, because she hadn't been alone in days. I'd upped the watch on her, leaving him with no opportunity to get to her. Thankfully, Clutch made sure he'd never get that opportunity.

When Clutch discovered Derek cowering in the apartment above Cass', he lost it. A fight ensued, and Clutch ended up shooting him— twice. He hadn't killed him, which gave me the opportunity to decide his fate. The brothers brought him to the clubhouse, where they anxiously waited for my arrival. Since Guardrail called, I'd been doing everything I could to get back home. Thankfully, Sara managed to pull some strings to get us a private flight into Washington.

Just before we boarded the plane, I walked over to Sara and said, "Thanks for this."

"Don't mention it. I'm just glad I could do something to help," she smiled. A concerned look crossed her face as she pleaded, "Be careful, Cotton."

"Always." I stepped forward and gave her a tight hug before I said, "Take care of yourself, Sara. I expect to hear from you... soon."

She nodded and watched as we loaded the plane, waving one last time before walking towards her car. Sara had really come through for us, and I was grateful. With her help, we were able to make it back to Washington before daybreak. When we walked into the clubhouse, Luke and Guardrail were waiting for us in the bar.

Luke immediately got up, walked over to me, and put his arms around me, hugging me tightly as he said, "Good to see you, man."

"Good to see you too."

He stepped back and smiled as he said, "Do you have any idea how hard it was to keep Mom from heading up there to see about you? She is not happy with you, bro."

"Didn't figure she would be, but there was no point in her coming all the way up there."

He laughed as he said, "Yeah, well, you try explaining that to her."

"I'll set her straight. Where's Derek?" I asked.

Guardrail stood up and said, "Stitch has him in the back. He's pretty bad off. Not sure how much longer he's going to make it."

"And Cass?"

"She's in the TV room. Had a hard night," he told me.

I knew I needed to tend to Derek, but he was going to have to wait. I needed to see Cass first, to see for myself she was really okay. Before I headed for the TV room, I turned to Guardrail and said, "I'll be there in ten."

He nodded as I walked out of the room and headed to find Cass. When I found her, I wasn't prepared for what I saw. She was curled up on the sofa, sleeping with her head on Clutch's shoulder. I was only standing there for a brief second when he looked up at me. He didn't move, just sat there, holding my Cass in his arms. I knew they were close. They'd been friends since the day she started working in the bar, but there was something different in the way he held her.

My chest tightened in anger as I looked at him holding her close. I wanted to jerk him up off that sofa and rip his fucking throat out, but instead, I walked out. I'd lost her, and I had no one to blame but myself. I needed time to think before I acted; I had learned that much. I stood outside in the empty parking lot, breathing in the early morning air, and tried to clear my head. Then the back door opened and there he stood. I didn't have to turn around to know it was Clutch. I could feel the uncertainty radiating off of him.

Without turning to face him, I asked, "How long?"

When he didn't answer, I turned around and said, "Dammit, Clutch. Answer the goddamn question! How long have you been in love with her?" I pushed.

I watched as he considered what he was going to say, and I could see he was struggling. Finally, he answered, "Honestly, I can't remember a time when I wasn't in love with her."

"Fuck," I roared.

He took a step forward and looked me right in the eye as he said, "I've never crossed that line, Cotton. You should know me better than that. I followed the orders I was given, and I was a friend to her. That's it."

"Fuck," I growled. "What the hell were you thinking?"

"I was following orders. As I always do. None of the other stuff matters. You saw the way she looked at you. We both did. She loves you, Cotton. Only you."

"Does she know?"

He shook his head and answered, "No. She has no idea."

Before I had chance to question him further, Guardrail opened the back door of the warehouse and said, "Everything okay out here?"

"Yeah. On our way inside," I told him as I stepped forward. When I walked inside the warehouse, my brothers were surrounding Derek, who was bound to a chair in the middle of the room. His head was slumped down with his chin resting on his chest, and he had two bullet wounds to the chest. I noticed the pool of blood beneath him and quickly realized Guardrail wasn't exaggerating when he said he didn't have much time left.

I walked over to Derek and grabbed a fistful of his hair, jerking his head back to face me. His eyes blinked open, and when he saw me, an evil smirk curled across his face. He took a struggled breath and mumbled, "I was wondering when you'd show up to the party."

"You're not looking so good, cousin," I smiled and released my grasp on his hair.

His eyes roamed over me, stopping when he saw the cane in my hand, and said, "Could say the same about you. Looks like I need to work on my fucking aim."

"Among other things. But you've been pretty fucking clever. How in the hell did you survive the crash?"

"Figured you thought I was dead. You've always been a gullible sonofabitch," he gasped, each breath more difficult than the last. "I was thrown from the truck just before it hit the bottom of the ravine. Guess you could say I had luck on my side."

As much as I appreciated that my brothers were there, having my back when I needed them, I had to do this on my own. I looked over to

Guardrail and motioned my head to the door as I said, "Out."

He nodded, and I watched as they all filed out the room. Once the door closed behind them, I turned my attention back to Derek. The color had completely drained from his face, and I could tell that his time was running short. I pulled a stool over and sat down in front of him as I said, "Looks like your luck's run out, Derek."

When he didn't answer, I said, "You know… you could've just left it alone. Gone on with your sorry fucking life and no one would have ever been the wiser, but you just couldn't do that, could you?"

He coughed, trying to muster up the strength to speak, then grumbled, "Fuck you."

"You've always wanted what you couldn't have. Just couldn't get it through your thick fucking head the club was never yours. Same goes for Sara. She never wanted you. Hell, she couldn't even stand the sight of you, especially after you tried to fucking rape her. But she wasn't enough… you had to go after Cass, too."

"Sara," he started. "She was something. Beautiful… Smart. But Cass. Fuck, she was a *real prize*." Blood started to trickle from the corner of his mouth as he said, "That girl has it all. Those legs and that mouth…. I was looking forward to having those lips wrapped around my cock right before I put a bullet in her head."

I jumped up from my stool and slammed my fist against the side of his jaw as I shouted, "Shut your goddamn mouth!"

I clenched my fists at my side and tried to steady my breath as I reined in my anger. I wanted to wrap my hand around his throat and end it right then and there, but I had to ask him, "Where was it going to end, Derek? When would it ever be enough for you?"

"Nothing… would ever be enough… Not even when everything you've ever wanted… everything you ever cared about was dead and buried," he snarled. "You did this to yourself, Cotton… You got greedy… Took what should've been *mine*."

"The club was never yours, Derek. You made sure of that long before I ever stepped in. Uncle Saul tried…," I started.

"*Fuck Saul*," he grumbled angrily. His voice was low and hoarse as he said, "It was easy, you know… Just took the bolts out of the rear brake caliper and let Daddy Dearest do the rest… He never saw it coming."

He confirmed what I'd always suspected, and the rage I felt was all-consuming. I reared back and punched him again and again, until his body fell limp in the chair. I looked down at my blood-soaked hands and knew down in my gut that it was over. I couldn't change the past. What was done, was done. I sat back down in front of him and watched as he struggled to breathe. He tried to fight it, tried to hold on, but it was useless. It took almost an hour for the life to completely drain out of him, and even after he was gone, I sat with him, trying to make peace with every-thing that had happened between us. But I finally realized that time might never come. I eventually got up and walked out of the warehouse, leaving Derek and our past behind me.

As soon as I stepped outside, Maverick walked over to me and placed his hand on my shoulder as he said, "We thought he was dead, Cotton. I fucked up…."

"Don't. No way either of you could've known he was thrown from that damn truck. Besides, doubt I'd be here right now if you hadn't gotten me to the hospital when you did. Derek's gone now. That's all that matters," I assured him.

"I'll get Derek sorted," he told me.

I nodded and without saying another word, I headed for the clubhouse. I knew my mother would be pissed I hadn't come to see her, but I couldn't face her. I hadn't slept in over twenty-four hours, and after dealing with Derek, I need-ed some time to decompress and hopefully get some sleep. Before I reached my door, I spotted Cass standing at the end of the hall. She stood there, frozen, as she stared at me with surprise.

"Cotton?" she whispered. She took a step

closer and began crying as she said, "My god, you're really here... and you're standing... walking." I wanted to go to her, but I didn't move. I deserved to lose her, but everything in my body screamed she was mine.

"Cass," I said softly.

She moved a few steps toward me, but stopped herself. I could see the wheels spinning in her head as she looked at me. Finally, she said, "I've missed you... more than you know."

"I'm here. Not going anywhere."

"I want so much to go back to the days before you were shot. But, Cotton, how do I do that? How do I forget how you hurt me? Even after I've read all of your letters, I just don't know what I'm supposed to do."

"You give me a chance... a chance to prove to you I know what a mistake I made, and I will do everything I can to make it up to you. All I'm asking for is a chance."

Her eyes dropped to the ground, and then she said, "I'm not sure I have it in me to give you that chance." I felt like I'd been punched in the gut as I watched her turn and head back down the hall. I had to fight the urge to go after her, but I knew pushing her wouldn't resolve anything. I'd give her time, but I wasn't giving up. She would be mine again.

I stepped into my room and locked the door behind me. I took off my cut and jeans, and dropped to the bed, closing my eyes as I mulled over everything that had happened in the past thirty-six hours. Cass, Derek, my recovery… it was all just too much. Eventually, everything just became a blur, and I fell asleep and didn't wake up until the next afternoon. I got up and took a hot shower, then headed outside to have a smoke. When I stepped through the back door, several of the brothers were in the back parking lot, working on Maverick's bike. They were swapping out the passenger seat, so Dusty would have an easier time riding at the run.

Doc spotted me, came over to me, and laughed as he said, "Wondering when you were gonna come out of the cave."

"Ah… missing me, Doc?" I laughed.

"Yeah, like a corn on my big toe," he pestered. When he saw Dallas pull through the main gate, he smiled and said, "Oh… I guess you should know, the guys planned a welcome back dinner for you tonight, so the girls are all coming to help out."

"Looking forward to it."

It was Saturday, so Dallas brought Dusty along with her. He was staring out the window, and when he spotted us, he immediately started waving. As soon as she parked the car, he hopped out and ran over to me. With a big grin on his face, he said, "Hey Cot-en. You feeling bedder?"

"Yeah, Dusty. I'm feeling much better. It's good to see you, little man."

He smiled and said, "Did you know I get to ride wit' Mav'rick on his bike?"

"He told me you were going to ride with him. I think that's pretty cool," I chuckled.

He looked down at my cane then asked, "You gonna get to ride wit' us?"

"Not this time. But I'll be there, front and center, to see you off," I assured him.

"Okay. I'll ride wit' you next time," he told me, then turned and ran over to Maverick. As usual, he slammed into him, giving him one of his big hugs. We all laughed as Maverick tried his best not to fall backwards.

"Yo, Dusty. I've missed you, little brother," Maverick laughed.

Still clinging to Maverick's waist, Dusty said, "You've been gone too long, Mav'rick. That was longer than a couple of days. I asked Mom, and she said couple means two."

"Sorry about that, buddy. Took a little longer than I thought," Maverick explained.

Dusty finally released him, and after he gave him a quick smile, he shot off for the clubhouse and shouted, "I gotta find Wy-it."

Once he'd gone inside, Doc walked over to me and said, "It's good to have you back, Cotton. We've missed you around here."

"It's good to be back, brother."

We all headed into the bar, and once every-one had started drinking and talking among themselves, Guardrail turned to me and said, "Hope you don't mind, but the brothers and I did some work over at your place," Guardrail told me.

"Yeah? What kind of work?"

"Maverick talked to your doctor and got a list of equipment you'd need for your rehab. We got what you'd need and set it up in your basement."

"I appreciate that, brother. I wasn't looking forward to going to a fucking gym," I laughed. "But I'll do whatever it takes to get on my bike again."

He nodded and said, "It won't be much longer. You've come a long way."

I was about to take another drink of my beer when I noticed Cass standing at the end of the bar. I couldn't take my eyes off of her. Even though she was talking to Henley and Maverick, her focus was completely on me. Her hair was pulled back, revealing her gorgeous face, and I couldn't wait a minute more to have her in my arms. I stood up and made my way over to her. I could see by the look on her face that all of her doubts were raging inside of her. I wanted noth-ing more than to ease all of her uncertainties, but I knew it'd take time. Thankfully, time was on my side. I'd do whatever it took to make her mine, no matter how long I had to wait.

Chapter 18

CASSIDY

COTTON. HIS NAME alone was enough to make my head spin, and to make matters worse, he was walking toward me, looking like sex on a stick. Damn it. I wasn't ready. I needed more time. After our talk the day before, I wasn't prepared to see that lustful look in his eyes, and my willpower was fading... fast. I'd missed him so much, and seeing him standing there with all his sex appeal and charm wasn't helping matters one damn bit. I knew I needed to tell him to go to hell... tell him to turn around and leave me the hell alone. He'd hurt me, really hurt me, and I couldn't just jump back into things with him without some kind of resolve. But damn, it was so stinking hard. He was just too damn irresistible. My mind was thinking one thing, while my body was thinking something else entirely. Just one look from him, and all of my girlie bits were going nuts, making me want to jump his bones and spend the entire night making up for lost time.

No.

I wasn't going to give in… at least not yet.

"Cass," he smiled knowingly. Damn that sexy smile. Why? Why did he have to be so damn tempting? It wasn't fair, and deep down he knew it. He freaking knew what an effect he had on me, and it pissed me off.

"Cotton," I answered, with no smile given in return. Check one for Cassidy.

"Hey, Cotton," Henley smiled as she gave him a quick hug. "Glad you finally made it back home. We were all worried about you."

"Thanks, Henley. It's good to be back, and congratulations on the baby. You've made Maverick a very happy man," he smiled.

"Thanks! I'm pretty happy about it myself. Just think… a little Maverick running around. It's gonna be awesome."

"I'm sure it will," Cotton smiled. "Looking forward to it."

Everything was fine until he turned his focus back to me. His eyes locked on mine, and I felt my knees begin to weaken as he declared, "We need to talk."

I had every intention of telling him no. I did. The word was sitting right there on the tip of my tongue, but instead, I said, "Okay."

"Alone," he pushed. When I nodded, he took

my hand and started leading me down the hall. With every step I took, I tried to muster up the hurt, all the anger I'd felt towards him since the day he'd sent me away. By the time we'd reached his room, I'd managed to work myself into quite a frenzy.

When the door closed behind us, I crossed my arms and said, "Just so you know... no one has ever hurt me the way you did. *No one.*"

"I know I hurt you, and I'm sorry, Cass," he said softly. "You know you mean everything to me..."

I crossed my arms in defiance and said, "If I meant so much to you, why would you send me away like that? Why did you say all of those hateful things to me? And why would you let Sara, your ex-girlfriend, stay with you?"

He raked his hands through his hair, and with determination in his voice, he said, "I thought I was protecting you, Cass."

I threw my hands in the air and shouted, "That's such bullshit, Cotton! There was nothing to *protect* me from."

He stepped closer to me, just inches away, and said, "Tell me this. What would you have done if I'd lost the use of my legs and couldn't ever walk again?"

"I'd love you just the same. It wouldn't matter to me you couldn't walk as long as you were with me."

"You're twenty-seven years old, Cass. You're going to tell me it wouldn't matter I couldn't have sex with you… or have kids with you? That I'd be bound to a fucking wheelchair and lose my presidency with the club? That wouldn't have mattered to you?" he asked.

"No. It wouldn't," I said defensively. "I love you, Cotton. We'd figure it out. If we wanted to have kids, we could have adopted or tried in vitro. Whatever it took. And being President of the club isn't who you are, it's what you do. You are the only thing I care about."

"You wanted to know why I did it. This is why I did it. I knew you'd sacrifice your life to be in mine. I couldn't do that to you," he explained.

"Well, it was an asshole move," I snapped. "You don't get to make decisions like that for me."

He placed his hand on my hip and said, "I know I hurt you, and I'll spend the rest of my life making it up to you."

"I'm not sure if that will ever happen… but you can try," I smiled. Maybe I was a fool for giving in so easily, but I didn't care. I wanted him. I'd always wanted him, and I was done fighting it.

"I've missed you," I whispered as my fingers drifted to his neck and tangled in his hair.

He leaned over me as he claimed my mouth, pressing his body into mine while his arm wrapped around my waist. Just being close to him again made me feel whole… safe and protected. I loved him, more than I ever thought possible, and I knew I was exactly where I was meant to be. A little moan escaped my lungs as the stubble of his beard brushed across my skin. His kisses trailed along my neck, sending chills throughout my body as he carefully led me over to the bed. Once he'd lowered himself to the bed, I rested both of my knees at his side, straddling him as we continued to kiss. I eagerly reached for the hem of his t-shirt, gently pulling it over his head before removing my own and tossing it to the floor.

He gently slipped my bra strap down my shoulder, and his kisses followed his touch as he pulled my breast free, gently caressing it in his hand. My head fell back as he began to nip and suck at the sensitive flesh, sending jolts of pleasure down my spine as he tormented my nipple with his mouth. The warmth of his breath caressed my skin when he whispered, "You're mine, Cass. You've always been *mine*."

Impatience overcame me, forcing me off of the bed to remove my jeans and panties. After I tossed them on the floor, I went back over to Cotton and gave his chest a light shove, signaling him to fall back on the bed. He smiled mischievously as he leaned back on the mattress. Once I unbuckled his belt, he lifted his hips just long enough for me to free him from his jeans. I'd barely gotten them off of him when he reached for me, pulling me back over on top of him. I rested my knees at his side like I'd done before, and a low growl vibrated through his chest as soon as his erection brushed against me. He looked up at me, and I could feel the heat of his gaze as his eyes roamed over my naked body. His hands snaked over my hips and up my chest as he reached for my breasts, squeezing them gently in the palm of his hands, while I rocked my hips back and forth, rubbing my clit against the head of his cock.

"Fuck," he groaned as he dug his fingers into my flesh.

The anticipation of having him inside me was almost too much to bear, so I reached beneath me, taking his long, thick shaft in my hand. I slowly stroked him up and down before positioning him at my entrance. With one swift thrust, he slipped deep inside me, giving me every inch of his bulging cock. I stilled for a moment, trying to adjust to his invasion before I started to move my hips again, quickly finding the spot that drove me wild. I leaned over him, pressing my lips against his, and his hand instinctively reached for the back of my neck, grasping at the hair around the nape of my neck and holding me in place as he deepened the kiss. I moaned into his mouth as his hips began to buck forward, thrusting his cock deeper inside me as he explored my mouth with his tongue.

My breath caught when I heard him whisper, "I love you, Cass."

I saw the emotion cross his face as he said the words I'd longed to hear, and I had no doubt he meant every word. I looked down at him, seeing nothing but pure love in his eyes, and said, "I love you too. With all of my heart and soul."

He placed his hands on my hips as I slowly began to move, groaning at the jolts of pleasure that shot through me. Each shift forward sent me closer to the edge. I pushed against him, forcing him further inside me, and bit my bottom lip in sweet agony when I felt the trembles of my impending orgasm. His fingers dug into my hips as he guided me back and forth, over and over again, until I reached a demanding pace. I placed my hands on his chest, trying to steady myself as I tried to maintain the relentless rhythm he'd set. My body trembled with anticipation when I felt my climax building, burning through my veins.

His breath quickened as I tightened around his cock, and I could see he was struggling to maintain his control. Panting and gasping for breath, I was ready to lose control as my muscles began to quiver. He put his hands under my ass, lifting me higher as he angled inside me, finding the spot he knew would send me over the edge.

"Yes!" I cried out and dug my nails into his

chest. My eyes clamped shut as my orgasm surged through my body. A loud, torturous growl escaped him as my body shook with violent tremors. I was lost in my own intoxicating pleasure when he finally found his own release. His brows furrowed as he thrust forcefully into me one last time.

I lowered myself on top of him, resting my head on his chest as I listened to our erratic breathing slow into a steady rhythm. Goosebumps rose on my skin when his lips brushed across my shoulder and along the curve of my neck. When he reached my ear, he whispered, *"Mine."*

Chapter 19

COTTON

"AS MUCH AS I love lying here with you, we've got to get up," Cass said softly. "The guys are expecting you at the party."

"Five more minutes."

"Okay, five more minutes," she agreed. "But then I have to get a shower and go help the girls get everything ready."

I pulled her closer, savoring the warmth of her body next to mine, and said, "We could just skip the whole thing. Spend the night right here."

"We could," she smiled. "I'd be okay with that."

"*But?*"

"*But* … you haven't even seen your mother and brothers yet, and the guys are really looking forward to welcoming you home. Everyone is bringing food and …"

"Okay… okay, we'll go," I conceded. "But when the party is over, we're going to the house."

"Your house?"

"Yeah, my house. We'll be staying there from now on." Her eyes flickered with confusion while she thought about what I'd just said. So damn cute. Before she had a chance to ask, I said, "When you get ready, I'll have the prospects go to your apartment and gather your things."

She immediately sat up in the bed and said, "Wait... what?"

"The way I see it... I have a whole lot of making up to do for hurting you like I did. Right?" I grinned.

"Um hmm."

"Well... it would be a whole lot easier if you were living with me while I did it." I knew it was fast, but if I learned anything from dealing with Derek, it was that I was done wasting time. I wanted Cass. I wanted a future with her, a family with her, and I was ready to get started.

Her eyebrows furrowed as she asked, "So you want me to move in with you?"

"Yeah. It makes sense. I figure it will take a lot of work, a lot of long, sleepless nights to make you forgive me, so it would be easier on both of us if you moved in," I chuckled.

"This isn't funny, Cotton. This is big. You've just asked me to move in with you!"

"I wasn't exactly asking... more like explaining why you are in fact moving in with me," I smirked.

"Oh, is that right?" she said sarcastically.

I nodded and said, "Yeah, that's right. I told you… you're mine. I take care of what's mine. And Cass, I plan on taking *very* good care of you."

She sat there, staring at me with wide eyes as she mulled over everything I'd said. It looked like she was about to say something, but she was interrupted when someone knocked on my door.

"Cotton?" Joe called through the door. "Mom's out front and wants to see you."

"I'll be out in a minute," I grumbled. I wasn't looking forward to the lecture I was going to get from her. I knew she wanted to come see me, especially when I'd first been shot, but having her there, worrying over me, wasn't going to help matters.

"Looks like you've got more making up to do," Cass laughed.

"You're right about that," I chuckled. "But with you… I'm just getting started."

She rolled her eyes and smiled, "Whatever… You just smile that sexy smile of yours and all is forgiven."

"Sexy, huh?" I teased.

"Yeah… you know you are, so stop teasing me," she scolded.

"Can't help myself." I nodded over to my luggage in the corner of the room and said, "I've got something for you over in my bag."

Her eyes sparkled with anticipation as she glanced over at my bag and asked, "What do you mean? A present?"

"Go over and see. It's in the top zipper," I told her. Trying to contain her excitement, she eased off the bed and walked over to my luggage. The hem of my t-shirt barely covered her bare ass as she bent over to retrieve the envelope from my bag.

Once she had it in her hand, she turned to me and asked, "Is this it?"

"Yep. Open it up."

Her fingers carefully tore at the seam of the envelope, and when it was finally open, she remained completely silent as her eyes roamed over the tickets. We all knew how much she loved Norah Jones, and I'd managed to score some tickets to a small concert she was doing in New York City at the end of the month. I watched her eyes fill up with tears as she gazed down at the tickets, and my heart leapt when she looked over to me and said, "I can't believe you did this. We're really going to New York to see Norah?"

"Yeah, baby, we are."

"You didn't have to do this," she cried.

I sat up on the bed and said, "I wanted to, Cass. I meant it when I said I'm going to do whatever it takes to make you happy."

She walked over to the edge of the bed, kneeling down between my legs, and said, "Well, you've made me happy. *Very happy* in fact. And not because of the tickets. Having you here, like this, is all I need to be happy."

I pressed my lips to hers, kissing her briefly before I said, "I'm here, and I'm not going anywhere."

"Good, now let's go. We've got to get moving. Your mother is waiting."

I groaned and said, "Don't remind me."

She stood up and smiled as she said, "Just remember that smile, and you'll be fine."

Cass got up, and I followed her into the bathroom. After we took a not-so-quick shower together, we both got dressed. Cass still needed to go to her room to finish getting ready, and when she opened my door to leave, my mother was standing on the other side. She smiled and said, "When you didn't come out to the bar, I thought I'd come check on you."

"Um hmm," I mumbled. "About to head that way now."

Cass looked over to me, her cheeks blushing with embarrassment, and said, "I better go finish getting ready, so I can go help the girls in the kitchen."

"I just need a quick minute with Cotton, and then I'll be there to help out," my mother told her.

"Ok, I'll see you in a bit," Cass said as she stepped into the hall. She'd only taken a few steps when she turned back and asked, "Did you bring your famous potato casserole?"

"Of course, I did. I know how you love it," mom smiled. "And I also brought one of my turtle pies."

"Awesome! I can't wait," Cass told her as she headed toward her room.

Mom walked over to me and wrapped her arms around me, hugging me tightly as she said, "You had me so worried."

"I know, Mom. I hated to know you were so upset."

"Don't worry about that. I'm fine, but I would like to talk to you about something," she told me as she released me from her embrace and walked into my room. She sat down at my desk chair and watched me as I shut the door. Once I sat down on the edge of the bed, she looked at me intently, like she was searching her thoughts for the right words to say. Then she said, "You are so much like your father, Cotton. In so many ways."

"I'd say that's a good thing."

"Of course, it is. He was a good man, and I loved him with all of my heart. You know that losing him almost destroyed me. He'd always done everything for us, and I didn't know what to do without him. I was completely lost, but you made me realize we could make it without him. You had this strength and determination like I'd never seen in a child. You never gave up. You saved our family."

"It wasn't just me. Uncle Saul helped us a lot, Mom."

"Yes. Your Uncle helped us, but nothing like you did. The way you were there for your brothers..." Tears began to stream down her face as she continued, "When I heard you'd been shot, I was beside myself. I didn't know if I was going to lose you... I couldn't take it if I lost you, Cotton. I just couldn't do it. I wanted to come and see you, but I understood why you didn't want me to come. No man needs their meddling mother hovering over them, especially when they're the president of an MC. I get that. But I was afraid I wouldn't get a chance to tell you..." she cried. She took a deep breath, swallowing her tears as she said, "I just wanted you to know that I think you are a good man and a wonderful son. You're always looking out for us, and I love you so much for that. But now that you are back and you're okay, I want you to look after yourself."

"I'm not going anywhere, Mom. I know I scared you, but I'm fine."

She wiped the tears from her face and said, "You did scare me, but I can see you're alright now. I'm so glad you are home and doing so well... I noticed that when I saw that sweet

Cassidy in here, looking like I just caught her with her hand in the cookie jar."

"Mom," I groaned.

"I like her. I think you should make an honest woman out of her," she smirked.

"Planning on that."

Her eyes lit up as she said, "Ah... she has beautiful eyes and her skin is flawless. Can you imagine what beautiful children you two would have?"

I knew it. She couldn't make it through one conversation without bringing up grandchildren. I stood up as I said, "We'll see soon enough."

She looked like someone had just told her she'd won the fucking lottery as she walked out of my room, clapping her hands quietly as she pranced down the hall. Trying my best to ignore her, I closed my door and headed to the bar. All of the brothers were already there, talking amongst themselves and drinking when I walked in. I took the stool next to Guardrail and motioned over to Tristan, letting her know I needed a beer. She immediately brought one over, and as she sat it on the counter, she said, "Good to have you back."

I nodded then turned to Guardrail and said, "Everything set for the run?"

"Yeah. We're all set, and they're calling for good weather next weekend. Should be a good turnout."

"Appreciate you taking care of it," I told him.

"Maverick did most of the work. I just tied up some loose ends." He took a drink of his beer, then said, "Nitro has a new shipment coming in and needs our order."

"Have Stitch check our inventory and see what we need." Nitro was our long-time supplier, and I knew him well enough to know, when he got in a shipment, he wouldn't sit on it. If we needed to restock, we needed to act fast.

"I'll have him do it first thing tomorrow."

"Just let me know, and I'll make the call to Nitro. Need to discuss a few things with him while I'm at it."

We talked for over an hour, but didn't get much said with all the brothers coming by to welcome me back. Once everyone had said their hellos, we headed to the kitchen. The girls outdid themselves with dinner, serving everyone's favor- ite foods and drinks. They'd gone all out to make sure I knew they were glad I was back home. When everyone finished eating, we headed back into the bar for more drinking. The girls started picking songs on the jukebox, and it didn't take long for the party to really get going. When Cass hit the dance floor with Henley and Tristan, I couldn't take my eyes off her. As always, she completely captivated me with her absolute beauty. When a slow song came on, I knew it was my chance to rectify a mistake I'd made many months earlier. I walked over to the girls and reached for Cass, pulling her close to me as I started to dance with her.

"Are you seriously dancing with me?" Cass laughed.

"Looks like I am." She rested her head on my shoulder and followed my lead as I swayed across the dance floor. There was no fancy footwork or spectacular spins, but it was enough. She knew how I felt about dancing, everyone did, but for her, I would do just about anything.

When the song ended, an upbeat rhythm replaced the sweet melody we'd been dancing to, and I shook my head, letting her know there was no way I was dancing to that shit. She smiled and mouthed, 'Thank you' before she watched me walk back over to my spot at the bar.

I looked around the room. Everyone seemed to be having a good time dancing and drinking, and I was surprised when Clutch approached me and asked, "You got a minute?"

"I do," I told him. When he started walking toward the back door, I followed him. Once we were both outside, I asked, "What's on your mind?"

He shoved his hands into his coat pockets and said, "I wanted to let you know I'm heading out for a while."

I didn't have to ask why he wanted to leave. I knew it was because of Cass. I'd seen the way he'd looked at her, and even though I'd been angry he'd let it happen, in the end, I couldn't blame him for loving her. I'd fallen for her the minute she walked into the bar, so the fact he was telling me he needed to get away didn't surprise me. I didn't like it, but I understood his reasons for wanting to go.

"Where you headed?" I asked.

"No real destination in mind. Thinking about going down south for a bit. Take a few months to drive across country."

I crossed my arms as I asked, "You coming back?"

"The club is my life, Cotton. Not letting it go. Just need some time to clear my head, is all," he clarified.

"I can respect that. You gotta do what you gotta do. You have my support, but I have to ask. Are you planning to talk to Cass about this?"

He shook his head and answered, "Think it's best if I don't." He reached in the back pocket of his jeans and brought out a small, white envelope with Cass's name on it. He handed it over to me and said, "This is for her. It's up to you whether she gets it or not."

"I'll see that she does," I promised. "I expect you to touch base. Let us know you're okay while you're gone."

"I will. And thanks. You and this club... don't know what I would've done without you."

"This is your home, Clutch. Nothing's going to change that. The door's always open when you are ready. Take the time you need, and we'll be here when you get back."

He gave me a quick hug, then turned and headed for his bike. He started up the engine, and I watched as he pulled out of the parking lot. It was hard to see one of my brothers leave, but I had to trust that in time, he'd eventually find his way back. He was one of my brothers, and I'd consider him my family until the end.

Chapter 20

CASSIDY

I T WAS AN absolutely beautiful day. The sun was shining bright, and the temperature was perfect for riding. When Cotton told me it would be crowded, I had no idea it would be so packed. There were hundreds of bikes lining the streets, and even more people roaming around, talking on the sidewalks and visiting the different vendors. Music from the band was blaring as I searched through the crowd, looking for Cotton. I finally found him standing at the front and center of all the bikes, directing oncoming traffic and motioning bikers to their place in the line. When I looked at him, he seemed so happy, but I couldn't help but worry. He'd decided to leave his cane at home, telling me that lately, he only really needed it when he was tired, but I put it in the trunk of my car just in case he needed it later. I don't know why I bothered. He'd be too stubborn to use it. He wanted to be back to his old self, but he just wasn't there yet. I hated it. I saw the look in his eyes as he watched his brothers prepare for the ride, and my heart ached for him. He'd worked so hard, pushing himself to the limit every single day over the past week, but the doctor refused to give him the okay to ride, even for a little while. Even though it was killing him, I knew he'd be back on his bike soon enough, and then his life would be back to normal... well, as normal as life could be for Cotton.

I ran the tips of my fingers over Cotton's name on my property patch, remembering the expression on his face early that morning when he'd given it to me. He said he wanted me to wear it during the charity run so everyone would know I was his old lady. I laughed and told him with the way he acted, I didn't need a jacket for everyone to know. I smiled to myself as I thought about how his eyes gleamed with pride when he watched me pull the leather jacket from the box. He helped me put it on, then kissed me and reminded once again that I was his – in every way. I was completely lost in my thoughts until Henley walked up, nudging me with her shoulder as she stood next to me. I turned my head towards her and watched as her face lit up as soon as she noticed Maverick. When he noticed her standing there, he got off his bike and walked over to her. He had an intense look on his face as he leaned over her and said something only she could hear. Tears filled her eyes as a bright smile spread across her face while she listened to him. He placed the palm of his hand on her belly and gently kissed her before heading back over to Dusty. By the time he got reached him, Dusty was about to burst with excitement. He watched as Maverick got on the bike, and anyone could see by the huge smile on his face that Dusty was thrilled he was going to get to ride with him. I laughed to myself when I noticed a similar smile on Maverick's face. Dusty was a lucky little boy.

Henley motioned over to Dallas as she said, "She looks a little anxious."

"She's just a little overwhelmed. This is a lot. All these people and not having Skid here to share it with her has to be hard on her."

"I'm sure it is, but she'd never say anything."

We watched as she went over to Dusty and secured his helmet before helping him onto Maverick's bike. Her eyebrows cinched together as she leaned over him, explaining once again about all the rules of riding. He nodded his head as he listened to her, and as soon as Maverick started the engine, she stepped back and watched Dusty put his arms around Maverick's waist. Dallas smiled at them and then started back toward the crowd. Henley was about to call out to her, but stopped when she saw that Dallas' parents were standing at the edge of the sidewalk, waiting for her.

Seconds later, all the different engines roared to life as they prepared to leave. The sound was almost deafening when several of the bikers revved their engines and started inching forward. Cotton eased to the side as he waved them forward, signaling them to begin their journey toward Olympic State Park. They had five stops, each one with its own theme, and it would take them most of the day to complete. The final stop was the clubhouse, where a huge party had been planned for everyone who participated in the run. While Cotton went with Doc to check out the first couple of stops, I went back to the clubhouse with Henley to finish getting things ready for the party. All of the cooking had already been taken care of, so when we got to the kitchen, there wasn't much left for us to do.

We were walking toward the bar to restock when Henley yawned and said, "Mind if I go take a nap? I'm wiped."

"Sure. I've just got a few things to put in the cooler anyway. You go get some rest," I told her.

"I won't be long. Just need a power nap," she yawned again.

I could tell by looking at her that she needed more than a quick rest, so I said, "The guys won't be back for hours. Take your time."

"Thanks, Sis. Holler if you need me," she told me as she headed down the hall toward Maverick's room.

The bar was completely empty, making me feel a little lonesome as I started filling the cooler with beer. I'd unloaded three cases when my curiosity finally got the best of me. I'd had Clutch's letter for almost a week. Cotton had given it to me the night he'd left, but I was too hurt, too angry to even consider reading it at the time. Clutch had been such a wonderful friend, and I couldn't imagine why he'd leave without saying anything to me. I needed to know, and the only way I was ever going to know was to read the letter he'd written. I reached into my purse, pulled out the small, white envelope, and opened it. I stared at the words for several minutes before I actually read what they said.

Hey there, beautiful,

I guess you're pretty upset with me right now. Can't say that I blame you. I wanted to come to you and tell you I was leaving, but I knew you'd ask me to stay. I couldn't take the risk. I knew if you asked me not to leave, I'd never have the strength to go. I needed to do this, Cass. I screwed up. I fell for the wrong girl.

I always thought it was funny how you thought I had all these women I was stringing along, but I never did. Since the day I met you, there's been no one who could hold a candle to you. I knew you were in love with Cotton, but I kept lying to myself. I kept telling myself it didn't matter, that being your friend was enough to get me by, but I was wrong. I couldn't do it, and now I have to find a way to make peace with the fact I can't have you.

Cotton's a good man. He loves you, and I know he'll do whatever it takes to make you happy. I want that for you. I want you to have all the happiness in the world, so don't let me down. Keep smiling that beautiful smile, keep singing those amazing songs you sing, and keep making the world turn on its axis every time you walk into a room.

I'll be back someday, but for now, I want you to know that I love you. A part of me always will. Forgive me for leaving like this and please try to understand why I had to go.

Clutch

I didn't know. I felt like such an idiot, but I just didn't know. Guilt washed over me as I stared at the words written in the letter, and my lungs tightened as I began to cry. My eyes blurred with tears as I read over it again and again, feeling the pain in his heart as I read it, and I wanted to kick myself for not realizing I'd been hurting him. My heart was so wrapped up in Cotton that I never even realized Clutch had those kinds of feelings for me. I knew our friendship was different than most, but ... Damn. I was such an idiot. I hated myself for being so blind. Clutch meant the world to me, and my foolishness forced him away. I wanted to call him, plead with him to come back home, but I couldn't do that to him. He needed time away, and I had to respect him enough to give it to him.

It'd been almost an hour since I'd read the letter when Cotton walked into the bar. Even though I was no longer crying, the minute he saw my face, he knew something was wrong. He quickly locked the main door and started walking toward me, only stopping when he was standing directly in front of me, and asked, "What happened?"

I shook my head and said, "I'm fine, Cotton. I'm a total idiot, but I'm fine."

"Are you going to tell me why you've been crying?"

I pointed to the letter on the counter and said, "I finally read it. Did you know how he felt?"

"Not until recently, but yeah. I knew," he confessed. "Hit him hard. I hated he decided to leave, but I understood why he felt like he needed to go."

"Why didn't you tell me? Why didn't you let me know I was the reason he left?"

"Would it have changed anything?" he asked.

My eyes dropped to the floor as I answered, "No. Probably not, but I could've told him I was sorry."

"There's nothing for you to be sorry about,

Cass. Shit happens, and sometimes the heart wants what the heart can't have."

"It's not exactly that easy, and you know it."

"It's easy to love you, Cass. I wouldn't be surprised if there were others out there pining away after you. It's sad, really. I kind of feel sorry for them," he chuckled.

"Whatever," I laughed. "I guess I'll give them all a break while we're in New York."

"I guess you will," he chuckled. "I'm looking forward to having you all to myself for a little while."

"You always have me all to yourself. You make sure of that," I teased.

"What can I say? I like having you close." He glanced around the room, and when he was certain no one was around, he put one of his hands behind my neck as he pressed his mouth against mine. My lips parted in surprise as he backed me up against the bar. His tongue swept across my open lips before dipping seductively into my mouth. The kiss was urgent, and I was quickly becoming lost in the heat of his need. I gasped into his mouth when his hands grabbed my ass, pulling my hips closer to his. I could feel the growing bulge of his arousal even through his jeans. His mouth roamed over the curve of my neck, while his hands roamed restlessly over my body.

"Cotton…" I breathed as I glanced toward

the door.

"It's locked, baby," he murmured between kisses. His hand greedily moved under my shirt, caressing my breast over my bra. "Besides, no one will be here for hours."

I let my inhibitions fall away as my desire for him took over. I reached for his cotton t-shirt, pulling it from his body, and watched it fall to the floor. He grinned devilishly as I bit my lip and lifted my arms over my head. He hands went immediately to the hem of my long sleeved t-shirt and eased it over my head, tossing it quickly to the floor. His hands roamed over my bare skin, only stopping when he reached my breasts. His fingers slipped inside the cups of my bra, pulling my breasts free. I licked my lips in antici-pation as he leaned back, his eyes devouring me, and I couldn't stop myself from squirming in the heat of his stare. A low growl rumbled in his throat as his hands ran up my back and un-hooked my bra. My fingers gripped his shoulders as his head lowered to my nipple, his tongue flicking across the tip before his lips surrounded it and began sucking with gentle pressure. My breath quickened as he moved to my other breast, and a shiver ran over me when the cold air hit my nipple where his mouth had been.

He released my breast from his mouth, let-ting my bra drop uselessly to the floor, and took a step back, eagerly grabbing my waist as he turned me to face the counter. I felt him twirl his hand around the length of my hair, gently tugging it as he said, "*Hands,* Cass."

A rush of anticipation surged through my body as I placed my palms on the smooth, wooden counter and waited. Goosebumps prickled against my skin when I felt the intense heat of his body radiating against my naked back. He placed his hands on my outer thighs, and a small moan echoed through the room as his rough fingertips began to slide my skirt up. His thumbs hooked in the waist of my lace panties, and he dragged them slowly down to my ankles. As I stepped out of them, I felt his fingertips trail up the inside of my thighs. My breath caught as fingers slipped between my legs, circling my sensitive clit.

I heard the tinkle of his belt and the slide of his zipper, and I groaned with anticipation, while he continued to torment me with his fingers. Even though I knew the door was locked, there was an extra thrill to being out in the open like we were, and the thought of getting caught only excited me more. Suddenly, I felt his thick erection slide between my legs as one of his hands grabbed my hip. He reached between us and positioned himself at my entrance before thrusting inside of me in one hard, smooth stroke.

A hiss escaped his lips as my body squeezed around him, adjusting to the fullness. I moaned in pleasure, relishing the feeling of him buried inside of me. His hands reached up to cup my breasts as he began shallow thrusts, readying me. He rolled his hips in an anguishing rhythm as my fingers grasped at the counter in desperation. His hands moved down to still my hips as he began driving into me with longer, deeper strokes. My body trembled and my breathing became ragged when my climax approached. I gasped as one of his hands reached around to tease my clit. The gentle pressure of his finger overwhelmed me and sent me over the edge.

"Don't stop," I cried while the waves of ecstasy rolled through my body. The pleasure was so intense, my legs momentarily buckled. His strong hands gripped my hips and held me upright as my body contracted around his hard cock. My muscles struggled to push him out, but his thrusts were relentless as he quickened his pace, chasing his own release. I began to rock my hips back into his, wanting him to be as satisfied as I was. I felt his cock swell inside me when he reached his orgasm. His growl echoed in the room as his rhythm slowed.

"I'll never get enough of you," he whispered in my ear.

"I'm good with that," I laughed and turned to face him. I wound my arms around his neck and said, "I love you, Cotton."

"I love you more," he said as he kissed me again and again.

Epilogue

Several Years Later

I'D LEFT THE house before daybreak, before Cass had even gotten out of bed, and spent the morning out on the bike. It'd been a long week, and I needed an hour to myself. As soon as I rolled the throttle back, my mind went blank and I was completely focused on the twists and turns of the road. There was truly nothing like feeling the wind in my face and the sun at my back. It was all the therapy I needed. I could've spent the entire day just riding. After I'd gone by the clubhouse to check in with Guardrail, I headed out to Cape Flattery to do some exploring. The smell of the salt air helped clear my thoughts, soothed my soul, as I rode along the coastline, and I was just about to pick up the speed when I felt my phone vibrating at my chest. I pulled over onto the shoulder, and when I looked down at the screen, I saw it was Cass calling.

I killed the engine, and as soon as I answered,

she said, "You have to do something about the girls."

Laughing, I said, "What are they up to now?"

"The usual," she huffed. "They've been going at it since they woke up."

I looked down at my watch, and when I saw that it was only eight, I asked, "How long have they been up?"

She sighed as she said, "About twenty minutes."

"I'll be home in ten."

"Cotton?" she whispered in that sweet, loving voice she got when she wanted something.

"Yeah, darlin'. Whatcha need?"

"Can you grab some milk on your way home?"

"Yeah, no problem. Need anything else?"

"Just you," she teased.

"You got me. I'll be there as soon as I can," I told her.

I didn't waste any time getting back to the house. I parked the bike and went inside, finding the house to be oddly quiet. When I walked into the kitchen, the refrigerator door was open and Cass was standing there, staring inside. She was still in her long, pink nightgown, and her hair was twisted on top of her head in a messy bun. She looked absolutely stunning as she ran her hands over her round belly. I dropped the bag of milk along with a few extras I'd bought on the kitchen counter, then walked over to her, gently kissing her on the back of the neck.

She leaned against me as she turned her head back toward me and said, "I forgot to tell you to grab some eggs, too."

"I got some," I smiled. "What's going on with the girls?"

She tucked a loose strand of her hair behind her ear as she said, "I may have overreacted. I woke up a little grumpy this morning. Your son is making it almost impossible for me to sleep, so I was a little on edge this morning. I shouldn't have called you to come home."

"When it comes to my girls, always call." I eased her away from the door of the refrigerator, then closed it as I said, "Now, go get in bed and get some rest. I'll see about the girls then I'll make breakfast. You sleep."

"You sure?"

"Absolutely. Now, go get some rest. I'll bring you a plate when it's ready."

She kissed me on the cheek and said, "Fore-warning... Darby pulled all the heads off of Susana's Barbie dolls and she's hidden them somewhere in their room."

I couldn't hold back my smile. Just like when I was a kid, my girls were always into something. Hiding the heads was a new twist for Darby, but I wasn't surprised she'd done it. For a six-year-old, she was pretty crafty with her revenge. But I knew she wouldn't have touched Susana's dolls unless there was a reason. I'd just have to figure out why she'd done it, so I assured Cass by saying, "I've got it under control."

I knew the twins were a handful, and seeing that Cass was eight and half months pregnant, she was feeling a little overwhelmed. When I walked into the room, Darby's curly hair was an untamed mess, while Susana's had already been brushed and pulled back into a ponytail. They were twins, but totally opposite in almost every way. Each was amazing in her own way, and I couldn't adore them more. When I walked into their room, Darby was sitting on her bed, playing with the cat, and when she looked up at me with those dark brown eyes, it was hard to imagine she could ever do anything as mischievous as taking her sister's dolls and mutilating them. Susana was sitting on the floor, pouting. When she spotted me, she immediately started with the waterworks.

Big, fat crocodile tears pooled in her eyes and ran down her chubby, little cheeks as she said, "Darby hurt my dollies."

I closed the door and crossed my arms, giving them both my best 'I'm not messing around' pose. Sometimes, that's all it took to get them to spill the beans on everything that had happened, but not today. They both just looked at me, giving me their most innocent expressions. Too fucking cute. I walked over to Darby's bed and sat down as I asked, "Why do you think she did that, Susana?"

"Cause she's mean," she answered as she glared over at her sister.

"I am not!" Darby barked. "You're the one who used up all of my smell-good soap in the bathtub last night. Momma gave that to me for my birthday."

"Did not!"

"Yes, you did. It's all gone," Darby grumbled. "Daddy, I told her to stop using my stuff."

I knew it had to be something. Darby was very picky about her things. Cass was always saying she was OCD about it, but I just thought it was cute. The kid took pride in her things, and I couldn't blame her for getting upset that her sister had taken something that was hers without asking. Susana reminded me so much of my brother, Luke. He was always getting into my stuff, even though he knew I'd give him hell about it. I remember a day when I was bitchin' to my dad about it, and he gave me a different take on things. He reminded me I was the older brother and Luke looked up to me. He thought my stuff was better, simply because it was mine. Although my girls were the same age, I figured it was a similar situation. I imagined Susana felt the same way about Darby's stuff as Luke felt about mine. I looked over to Susana and asked, "Susana, why did you take her stuff without asking?"

"Cause I knew she'd say no, and I just wanted to use a little. It smells really good..." she admitted. She looked down at her hands and whispered, "I'm sorry, Darby."

I turned my attention back to Darby and said, "You think you could accept your sister's apology and give her back her dolls?"

Darby scrunched up her eyebrows as she said, "But Daddy... she used it all, it's gone. It's not fair."

"It's soap, Darby... we can get some more. Your sister likes your things. You should take it as a compliment."

Her face softened as she looked over at her sister. She took a moment to think before she asked, "If I give you back your dolls, are you gonna leave my stuff alone?"

"Or at least ask before you use it," I interjected.

"Yeah, I promise."

"And Darby," I warned. "Next time, tell me or your mother when something like this happens. Taking the heads off of your sister's dolls was wrong."

"I know. I'm sorry, Daddy" she told me as she got up from her bed and went over to her dresser. She pulled out her bottom drawer and reached in underneath all of her clothes, retrieving her sister's dolls.

"Susana, come here," I told her as I motioned for her to come over and sit on the bed next to me. Once she was curled up next to me, I reached for Darby, pulling her next to us and said, "You know, it won't be long before you brother gets here. You've got a big job ahead of you."

"What kind of job?" Darby asked.

"You've got to show him the ropes. Show him how things work in the world. I'm counting on you both to do right by each other, so he'll see how it's done."

"We will be good, Daddy," Susana assured me. "I won't take Darby's stuff anymore."

"And I won't hurt Susana's dolls or put bugs in her hair anymore."

I laughed as I said, "That would be a good start. My daddy always told me it's okay to make a mistake as long as you learn from them."

"Like that time Momma turned all your white shirts pink?" Darby asked. "She hasn't done that again."

"Yeah, kind of like that." I smiled.

"Momma said that Henley and Maverick were coming over today for Grandpa's birthday. Is Thomas coming, too?" Susana asked. Thomas was Maverick and Henley's son. He was a bit older than the girls and tended to use that to his advantage.

"Yeah, I reckon he is."

Susana got a serious expression on her face as she said, "He hasn't learned from his mistakes, Daddy. He gets in trouble every time he comes to play with us."

"We'll keep an eye on him. Just have fun with Lexi and Grandpa. Maverick and I will keep Thomas entertained in the garage." Lexi was Maverick and Henley's daughter. She was just a few months younger than our girls, so they usually got along better with her than Thomas.

"Okay," Darby answered.

"I'm going to make breakfast. Either of you want to help?" I asked.

"Can I stir the eggs?" they both asked at the same time.

"Yep," I told them while I kissed each of them on the forehead and started for the kitchen.

We spent the next half-hour making breakfast, and once it was all done, I made a plate and took it into the bedroom for Cass. She was propped up on a pillow, reading a book, and smiled when she saw me entering the room. She sat the book down in her lap and asked, "How did it go with the girls?"

"Got it sorted," I told her as I placed her breakfast down on the bedside table. "They have an unfair advantage, you know."

"Yeah? What's that?" she smiled.

"They're beautiful like their mother. Makes it hard to fuss at them," I told her as I leaned over and kissed her lightly on the lips.

"They may be beautiful, but they are a handful. Actually, I think they get that from you," she teased. "I was always a good child."

I shook my head with disbelief and said, "I'm sure you were a perfect angel."

"I mean... I had my moments," she confessed.

"Now the truth comes out. Something tells me you could give our girls a run for their money," I taunted.

"I don't know about that. Two to one... I wouldn't stand a chance," she laughed.

"I've got your back, baby." I kissed her once more and then said, "We've got this."

The End

Clutch's book will be released mid-summer.

There will also be more from Sara in a future series.

Acknowledgements

Followed by a short excerpt of Stitch

I don't know where to start. With each book, I am more and more thankful for the people in my life who make this journey possible for me. My family has been an incredible support, and I wouldn't have been able to do it without them. My mother continues to be my rock, and I appreciate her more than she will ever know.

Amanda Faulkner has also been a huge blessing to me. I've never known how much help a PA could be until the day she stepped into my life. I have been blown away by all the support and the friendship she has given me over the past year. She has such a positive outlook and keeps me going whenever I need a push. Her partner in crime, Natalie Weston, has also been a huge help to me. I can't thank either them enough for all they do to promote my books and just being there whenever I need them. Thank you, Amanda and Natalie.

Danielle Deraney Palumbo continues to amaze me. Even when things get tough, she always finds a way to face things head-on, and she does it with a great attitude and a funny story to boot. Whenever I am having doubts, she finds a way to put me on the right track and help me get my books where they need to be. Thank you, Danielle, for taking the time out of your busy life to help me. I appreciate it more than you know.

I also want to thank Marci Ponce for all of her help with Cotton and the Satan's Fury series. She has such great insight when it comes to MC romances, and her help over the past year has been invaluable to me. I am excited about her venture to start her own series with the Forsaken Saints. I am sure it will be amazing, and I can't wait for her to get started. Thank you, Marci.

I am so excited to be working with Julia Goda. When I messaged her about editing my new series, I knew right away she was going to be awesome to work with. She took the time to go back and edit Maverick and the other books in the Satan's Fury MC series, making them all even better, and I can't thank her enough for taking the time to edit Cotton.

I would also like to thank all of my readers. I have loved all of your comments and posts. It means so much to me to hear you have enjoyed reading one of my books. You have all been so supportive, and your comments always leave a smile on my face. When my life gets a little crazy, your kind words have given me the encouragement I've needed to continue on. Thank you, Leah Joslin, for being there to make me smile and encourage me when things get hectic. It has meant such much to me. You rock!

My Wilder's Women Street Rocks!!! Thank you all for your support. It means so much to me that you continue to help me with reviews and posting all of my teasers. You all are such a huge help to me. I am always amazed each time I see one of my teasers or my links they have shared. Thank you for taking your time to help me. It means more than you will ever know.

Another special thank you goes to Sue Banner. From the start, she has shown me so much kindness, and it has meant so much to me. She takes time out of her busy schedule to help make sure the book is ready for you, and she does an amazing job. She also beta/proof reads for her son's books. If you haven't had a chance to check out Daryl Banner's books, you are missing out.

www.facebook.com/DarylBannerWriter

tinyurl.com/pzogl4p

Ana Rosso, my little grasshopper, thank you for always being there to read all the various editions of my books, making sure I get it just right. Even though you are hundreds of miles away, you are like my personal cheerleader. I hope to do the same for you when your new book releases! Can't wait! Keep on rocking, chickaroo!!

STITCH

Satan's Fury MC

Book 2

Satan's Fury MC
Copyright © 2015 L Wilder

All rights reserved. Without limiting the rights under copyright reserved above, no part of this publication or any part of this series may be reproduced without the prior written permission of both the copyright owner and the above publisher of this book.

This book is a work of fiction. Some of the places named in the book are actual places. The names, characters, brands, and incidents are either the product of the author's imagination or are used fictitiously. The author acknowledges the trademarked status and owners of various products and locations referenced in this work of fiction, which have been used without permission. The publication or use of these trademarks is not authorized, associated with, or sponsored by the trademark owners.

Warning: This book is intended for readers 18 years or older due to bad language, violence, and explicit sex scenes.

Editor – Marci Ponce
Levi Stocke
www.facebook.com/levi.stocke

Photographer – Mariusz Jeglinski
www.facebook.com/mariusz.jeglinski
mariuszjeglinski.com

Prologue

"HUSH, LITTLE BABY, don't say a word. Mama's gonna buy you a mockingbird. If that mockingbird don't sing, Mama's gonna buy you a diamond ring," my grandmother sang. Her voice was low and soft, and I finally started to calm down after another one of my nightmares. They started shortly after I moved in with my grandparents. I was eight years old when my parents were killed in a car crash, forcing my sister, Emerson, and me to move from the only home we'd ever known to live with my father's parents. We barely knew them, but they were the only relatives we had. I never knew how good we really had it until it was all ripped away. It had almost been a year, but I was still having a hard time adjusting to the change. That night, I'd made the mistake of accidentally wetting the bed. My grandmother held me close, trying to comfort me, while she continued to sing. I knew her words were a lie, that my mother was dead and gone, but listening to her soothed me. "If that diamond ring turns brass, Mama's gonna buy you a looking glass."

Pound.

Pound.

Pound.

His fist slammed against the wall as he walked toward my room. Horror washed over me as I listened to his footsteps coming down the hall. The floorboards creaked under the weight of his body, my dread intensifying with every step he took.

Closer.

Closer.

Closer.

My head was pressed against my grandmother's chest, listening to her heart thump rapidly while he started to shout, "Don't coddle that boy, Louise. Stop lying to him! His mama's dead. She can't buy him a damn thing! He's no fucking baby. We're not raising him to be a goddamn pussy!" he barked as he stood in the doorway with a scowl on his face.

"George," she started, but he quickly cut her off, raising his palm up in the air, silently ordering her to shut up. She always tried to get him to stop, but it never worked. Once he got it in his head, there was no changing his mind.

"Don't," she pleaded as I curled deeper into her lap when he started stalking toward me. With his finger pointed directly in my face, he growled,

"You wet that damn bed again, boy?" Rage vibrated off of him as he spoke, and I knew what was coming. He was furious, and only one thing happened when he got that worked up.

The barn.

My grandfather was a military man, born and bred. He still looked the part too, sporting his buzz cut and the same athletic build he had in all of his army pictures. Every minute of every day was controlled by his orders. He ran a tight ship with impossible expectations. The old man was a force to be reckoned with, and he hated any sign of weakness. Which meant he detested me. He hated that I was so weak, that my parents' deaths still tormented me. He was determined to make a man out of me, even if that meant killing me in the process. There was a time, when the beatings first started, when he was careful, not wanting to leave any evidence of the abuse. But as I grew older, he made sure to leave the marks. He got some kind of sick satisfaction, seeing the whelps on my back, smiling whenever he saw me looking at them. He wanted me to see them, to feel the raised scars on my flesh, so I would always remember. He grabbed my hand, yanking me from my grandmother's lap, and snarled, "Get your ass to the barn. I'll teach you not to wet the fucking bed, boy." I could smell the mix of old spice and bourbon swirl around me as my body collided against his side.

"George, it's late," Grandmother Louise pleaded.

Ignoring her, he pulled me out of the room and down the hall. As I stumbled behind him, I caught a glimpse of Emerson sitting up in her bed, tears streaming down her chubby little cheeks. She was only four years old, but she knew what happened out in the barn. Even though it sucked I was his main target, I was thankful he'd never taken her out there. The old man had a soft spot for her, and she could do no wrong. I wasn't resentful. I felt the same way about her.

My bare feet dragged along in the dirt and grass as he pulled me into the barn; the large, wooden doors slammed behind us, leaving us in the dark. The smell of straw and livestock whirled around me as he jerked me further into the dark. There was a time when I would try to pull away from him, but I quickly learned there was no use fighting him. I was trapped, unable to break free from his grasp. After binding my hands over my head, he reached for his favorite leather strap.

"If your father were still alive, he'd be disgusted with you. Such a fucking disappointment. You're just like your damn mother. Worthless," he grumbled as the strap whipped across my back. A searing pain shot through me, like hot coals burning through my thin t-shirt. I forced myself to hold back my cries as he continued to thrash the leather against my back, not wanting to give him the satisfaction of seeing me break. Unfortunately, that only made him angrier, causing him to hit even harder. Thankfully, it didn't take long for me to pass out from the pain, my body falling limp against the restraints.

There were many more nights like that, more than I could even begin to count. At least some were quick, not like the times he'd make me wait for it. I hated those nights the most. I'd spend the whole day tending to the animals and the grounds, praying the entire time he might forget about punishment he'd promised. He always remembered though. With a wicked smile on his face, he would pull me inside the barn, laughing whenever I pleaded with him to give me another chance. I would beg, promising to try harder... be better, more obedient, but he was completely unaffected. I soon learned it was pointless. He relished in the pain he inflicted on me; I could see it in the way his eyes would glaze over. It seemed my pleas were just a pre-game warm-up filling him with anticipation for the main event. He was one sick son-of-a-bitch.

Over time, I got stronger. I learned to take myself out of the moment, dreaming of the day I might be able to get away—the day I would be free from him. I was almost fifteen before that time finally came. That was the night he almost killed me. The night he decided to trade in his leather strap for a strand of barbed wire. As the metal spikes gouged into my back, he'd yank them free, ripping away my flesh. When he was done, he left me to bleed to death in one of the horse stalls. I had no idea how long I'd been lying there when Emerson managed to sneak out to help me. She tended to the wounds on my back and shoulders, crying the entire time. She pleaded with me to run away, to get away while I still could. I knew she was right. I didn't have a choice. I took the clothes and food she'd thrown in my backpack and left. I hated I had to leave Emerson behind. I wanted to take her with me, keep her close. But I knew Grandmother Louise would look after her and keep her safe, something my grandfather would never allow her to do for me.

I thought living on the streets would be better. I thought I'd be able to free myself from all the abuse, fear, and suffering my grandfather inflicted on me, but l was wrong. So fucking wrong. I'd only traded one hell for another. What my grandfather failed to teach me, I learned the hard way while living out on the streets. I was scared all the time, and starving most of the time. There was no one that I could trust; it seemed like everyone was out to get me. I had to be smarter and meaner than any of the filth that surrounded me. I stole. I fought. I even killed a guy—stabbed the son-of-a-bitch right in the throat when he tried to force himself on me.

The hunger, the fear, and the emptiness almost broke me. When I'd finally had enough, I decided to take the advice of a man who ran a halfway house down on the eastside. He was more decent than most and seemed to really care about the kids who came to him over and over. He told me that since I had managed to stay out of jail, there was a good chance I could join the military.

Despite how much I loathed my grandfather, I decided it was something I needed to do. Maybe it was to prove the old man wrong, show him I could face adversity and thrive. It was probably the same reason my father joined all those years ago, just to prove that bastard wrong. Regardless of the reason, I needed the stability the military could give me. I craved it, and being in the service was one of the best things I'd ever done. My troop became my family. We trained together... fought together. We became stronger, more disciplined together. It was the first time I had someone watching my back, caring whether I lived or died, and I was actually happy there. I figured I'd spend my life serving my country, but just when things were going well, everything fell apart. My platoon was transporting supplies to one of the neighboring villages when the lead carrier ran over a land mine. Soon after, the second carrier was ambushed, leaving most of my troop either dead or dismembered. It was a sight that will be forever burned into my memory. Seeing my brothers either dead or missing limbs broke something inside of me. The old hardness and coldness returned. Whatever weakness or compassion was left in me was wiped out that day. When I left the service, I was capable of doing unthinkable things, and I could do them without a touch of remorse.

They say your past defines you. I'd say they are right.

Chapter 1

WREN

"FIVE MORE MINUTES, and then it's time to finish up your homework and have dinner," I warned Wyatt. He looked so content, sitting at the end of the sofa with his little legs tucked underneath him. His fingers were rapidly tapping the screen as he worked diligently to create a new world on his video game. The things he could create on that little device always amazed me.

"But I'm just about to slay the dragon," he whined, never looking up from his game. His little nose crinkled into a pout at the thought of having to stop.

"Don't even start, mister. You know the rule." He'd been playing since we got home from school, and he'd keep playing all night if I let him.

"Okay. Five more minutes," he answered in defeat. His shaggy, brown hair dangled in front of his eyes, making me wonder how he could even see to play his game.

"Dude. I think it's time for a haircut."

He quickly ran his fingers through his bangs, brushing them to the side, and said, "No way! This is how it's supposed to look." He gave me a quick glare, his dark eyebrows furrowed in frustration before he looked back down at his game. Seeing him sitting there, I couldn't help but smile. He looked like your average eight-year-old boy with his wrinkled t-shirt and jeans, but to me, he was anything but average. I could see that Wyatt was an exceptional child, always marveling at all the wonders of the world. Every day, he'd share something new he had learned, eagerly telling me every single detail of what he'd discovered. I loved hearing the excitement in his voice when he spoke, flicking his wrists at his sides as he focused on what he was saying. I had no problem admitting that my entire world was wrapped up in that little boy and there was nothing better than seeing him happy.

"How about fish sticks for dinner?" I offered.

"Nah. I want chicken nuggets."

"Wyatt, you had those last night. You're going to turn into a chicken nugget one of these days," I laughed.

"That's physically impossible, Mom. Chickens are birds. People can't turn into birds," he fussed, shaking his head.

My child, always so literal. I smiled and said, "I know, buddy. I was just teasing. Are you set on chicken nuggets?"

"Yeah. I won't get them tomorrow night. Dad never has them at his house," he grumbled as he turned off his game. His brown hair fell into his face, hiding his look of disappointment. I cringed at the thought of him going to his dad's. He'd been going to his dad's every other Thursday for months, but it was still hard for him to transition from one house to the other. It also didn't help that I was terrified every time he had to go stay with his dad. I tried my best to hide my concerns from him, but I could tell he sensed something was wrong.

I started dating his father, Michael, when we were still in high school, and I absolutely adored him. I loved his strength and protectiveness, not to mention he was devastatingly handsome. He came from a good home and was extremely close to his parents, which I loved...at the time. I felt safe wrapped up in his arms, thinking that our love for each other would be enough to see us through anything. Back then, I really thought we'd spend the rest of our lives together. Unfortunately, the thing I loved the most about him ended up being the very thing that scared me the most about him. Over time, he became controlling and jealous to the point that I felt suffocated by him. I was nearly paralyzed by my inability to make a move without his approval. If I didn't do things the way he expected me to, he'd get angry, so very angry. His temper was a force to be reckoned with. When he snapped, I didn't know how to protect myself from his wrath. I'd tried everything, from talking him down with reason to silently enduring it. Nothing worked. I'd known about the fights he'd had at bars and various other places when his temper got out of hand, but I never thought he'd be like that with me. The first time I saw the flash of rage that crossed his face directed at me, I was stunned. I wasn't expecting him to be thrilled I had gotten pregnant so early in our marriage, but his intense anger caught me completely off-guard. I'll never forget the way he looked at me when he reared back his closed fist and slammed it into the side of my head. It was like he wasn't even the same person. That beating was so bad the doctor was surprised I didn't miscarry.

Michael cried for days afterwards, pleading with me to forgive him. He promised—he swore to me—that it would never happen again. Michael said he would do whatever it took to make our baby happy. I hadn't even finished college yet. If I left him, I would end up moving in with my parents and raising my child without a father. Truthfully, I loved my husband, and I wanted— no, I needed—to believe him. I had to trust him when he said he would take care of us and give us the life he'd promised. Even though I was only a few months pregnant, my child had already become the most important thing in the world to me. It's one of the reasons I named my son Wyatt, my little warrior. At the time, I had no idea how much the meaning of that name truly suited him.

In reflection, I should've left Michael that night and never looked back. But I honestly thought the incident would be a one-time thing. I told myself the shock and stress from the news of my unexpected pregnancy had just completely overwhelmed him and caused him to totally flip out. Unfortunately, I couldn't have been more wrong. The attacks were sporadic but effective. I never knew what was going to set him off, and over time, I became a different person. I hated that I didn't stand up for myself more, demand that he treated me better, but the fear was just so all-consuming. I eventually learned to do whatever I could to make him happy, always trying my best to keep the peace. I was finally learning to deal with Michael and his temper, but when we found out about Wyatt, things got worse.

As Wyatt got a little older, I became worried he wasn't talking like most of the children his age. When I finally took him to be tested, they informed us that he had Asperger's Syndrome, a form of autism that causes some children to have trouble with social interactions, and they often exhibit a restricted range of interests and repetitive behaviors. It was a heartbreaking discovery, but I still managed to remain hopeful. Wyatt was a wonderful little boy, and I loved him just the way he was. Unfortunately, Michael hated that his son was different. Image was everything to Michael. He was fixated on us appearing as the perfect all-American family, especially to his parents, and he blamed me for Wyatt's delays. Ultimately, I ended up in the hospital for five days with three cracked ribs, a broken wrist, and slight head trauma, all due to his frustration with our son. That night changed everything. I was done trying to make things work with an abusive husband. I gathered up all the courage I could muster and pressed charges against him. It's one of the reasons he now has supervised visitation with Wyatt and had to attend anger management classes for a year. The classes seemed to be helping him, but they didn't make me feel any better about sending Wyatt over there. I just don't trust Michael, but in the end, the courts left me no choice.

When Wyatt caught me staring at him, he asked, "So, are you going to make nuggets?"

"Yeah, I'll make chicken nuggets, but you're going to have to eat some vegetables, too," I told him as I headed toward the kitchen.

Wyatt reached for his backpack and followed

me, tossing his things on the floor by the table. "Okay, but no broccoli. I hate broccoli. And I got a one hundred on my math test today," he told me, pulling his books out and placing them on the kitchen table.

"That's great, buddy, but I'm not surprised. You always do well in math."

"It's my favorite," he confessed.

"I know. It was always mine too. Since you did so well, you can have a few extra minutes on your game after dinner."

As usual, I got no response. He knew he earned extra time on his game when he made good grades, so after dinner, he curled up in his favorite spot and finished creating his new world. When he was done, he headed for the shower without being told. I searched through his drawers, looking for his favorite pajamas, and laid them on his dresser. I sat down on the edge of his bed and waited for him to finish up in the bathroom. The shower turned off and seconds later, I heard Wyatt's wet, little feet slap against the hardwood floor as he headed down the hall. He stopped at the doorway and stared at me with one towel wrapped around his waist and another around his head.

"What's up, Buddy?" I asked.

"Nothing," he answered as he walked over to me and wrapped his little, wet arms around my neck. When I wrapped my arms around him, a mix of fruity shampoo and my favorite body wash surrounded me. I held him tight against my chest, kissing him lightly on the side of his head. I cherished those moments. Wyatt isn't one to give affection often, but when he does, there's no better feeling in the entire world. There was a time when he wouldn't even talk to me, much less touch me, so I held him close, enjoying the moment while it lasted.

"Time for bed, Momma," he told me, pulling free from my embrace. He reached for his clothes and started to get dressed, letting me know he didn't need my help.

"I'll be back in a few minutes to check on you," I told him as I got up and started to leave. "Love you, Buddy."

"You too," he replied while he crawled into the bed. I went back to check on him fifteen minutes later, and he was already sound asleep.

The next morning, Wyatt was already up and getting dressed by the time I had gotten out of the shower. When he finished getting ready, he stood at my bedroom door, sporting his favorite pair of red tennis shoes.

"Ready," he told me with a wide smile.

"Breakfast?" I asked.

"I got a granola bar."

"You know that's really just a snack, but I'll let it slide today," I said, playfully rolling my eyes at him "Want some juice or something?"

He shook his head no and headed out the front door toward the car. Overall, it was a great morning, and things continued to go well until I got to my last class of the day. I'd always wanted a career in family counseling and after my divorce, my parents encouraged me to go back to college to get my degree. They helped pay for my classes until my financial aid kicked in, and Mom helped with Wyatt when I was in class. I couldn't have done it without them, and things were going really well until I started my Counseling Theories class.

"I don't know how much more of this I can take," Rachel whined. "He has to be the most boring man on the planet."

"I feel ya, girl. I'm on my second cup of coffee, and I'm still having a hard time staying awake," I grumbled. I was just a few classes away from graduating, but first, I had to survive Professor Halliburton. Thankfully, I had Rachel there to keep things interesting. I'd met her last semester in my Crisis Management and Prevention class when she asked to borrow my notes, and we'd been friends ever since.

"It's his voice. Seriously, every time he opens his mouth, it's like nails on a chalkboard," she said, drawing out her words as she spoke.

Several heads turned and looked in our direction when we both started laughing. "You're a nut, Rach."

"Hey, you want to catch a movie after the gym tonight?"

"I wish I could, but I can't. Wyatt will be with his dad after school, so I'm going to try to run some errands." I wasn't exactly lying; I really did have lots to do. My laundry was piling up, and I had to get some studying done, but those weren't the reasons I didn't want to go. I knew I wouldn't be able to enjoy myself knowing Wyatt was with Michael.

"Wren, we both know why you don't want to go, but I get it. I know it's hard sending him over there."

"I'm sorry. I just get so anxious when he has to go over there. It's like I'm always waiting for the other shoe to drop," I explained.

"I can only imagine. It has to be just as hard for Wyatt," Rachel told me.

"It is, but at least he has Mrs. Daniels. I don't know what I'd do without her. She's really good with him."

During our divorce, Michael fought hard for joint custody of Wyatt. Sadly, it had nothing to do with being with Wyatt. No, it was just another way for him to try to hurt me, to exert his control over me. He thought he was being so clever, but I knew exactly what he was doing. His random calls to check in on his son were never about Wyatt. It was just Michael's chance to interrogate Wyatt on what I was doing or where

I'd been. Pushing for joint custody was just his vindictive way to get my child support reduced, knowing full well that less money would make it difficult for me to make it on my own. It was all just a ploy to make me miserable, and it was working. I didn't feel like I was making any progress, until I found Mrs. Daniels. The judge suggested her independent service company for Michael's supervised visitation, knowing they had experience working with children with special needs. With Mrs. Daniels' background, she knew what to expect with Wyatt's Asperger's. He was high functioning, but dealing with all of his little quirks could still be difficult.

"He's lucky to have her. You both are," she said, smiling. "I'll tell you what... why don't we hit the movies this weekend? We can take the kids with us and grab a pizza after."

"That sounds great. Wyatt loves Annalise, and he's been wanting to see that new Charlie Brown movie."

"Great! It's a plan then. Having something to look forward to might help me get through the next thirty minutes of Dr. Boring," Rachel said, laughing.

After class, we both headed over to the gym for self-defense training. Rachel was a little hesitant about taking the class until she met the instructor, Brandon. Even though she spent most of the hour gawking at him, it was nice to have her there with me.

"Is it just me, or does Brandon look like Joe Manganiello?" Rachel asked as we were walking out of the gym.

"Hmmm... no. Not even close," I told her, laughing.

"Yeah, well, he probably has a girlfriend anyway."

"For a guy with a girlfriend, he certainly keeps his eyes trained on you," I told her as my phone began to vibrate in my duffle bag.

"Really? He looks at me?" she asked, like she didn't know what I was talking about.

"All the time," I told her, looking down at my phone. My heart dropped when I noticed I had three missed calls from Mrs. Daniels. "Shit. Mrs. Daniels has been trying to call me." I dialed her number and prayed she would answer.

"Wren?" Mrs. Daniels asked.

"Yes, it's me. Is everything alright?"

"I tried calling earlier, but I couldn't get through to you. I knew you had your class tonight, but no one answered the phone there either. I wouldn't have left, but I didn't have a choice when I couldn't get in touch with you," she explained.

"Left? What do you mean?" I asked, feeling the panic begin to grow in the pit of my stomach.

"My husband was taken to the hospital, Wren. I called one of my associates, and she is on the way over to Michael's house now to see about Wyatt. Everything should be okay, but I wanted you to know what was going on."

"Wyatt's there alone with Michael?"

"Just until Anita can get there. He was fine when I left. Michael was finishing up some work on his computer, and Wyatt was playing one of his video games." She paused for just a second before she continued, "Wren, you know I wouldn't have left him unless it was an emergency."

"I completely understand. I'm on my way over there right now to make sure everything is okay," I told her. "Thanks for calling to let me know."

"Let me know if there is a problem. I will call Anita and let her know you are coming."

"Thanks," I told her as I hung up the phone. "I've got to head over to Michael's and make sure Wyatt's okay!"

"Why? What's going on?"

"Mrs. Daniels had an emergency and had to leave," my voice trembled. I fought back my tears as I started walking toward my car.

Following close behind me, Rachel asked, "Do you want me to go with you? You don't need to be driving when you're upset like this."

"No. I'll be fine. I just need to get over there," I explained as I got in my car and started the engine. I didn't have time to explain why having her there would only make it harder. Michael wouldn't be happy about me showing up there early, and having someone with me would only make it worse.

My mind raced with a million awful thoughts as I pressed my foot against the accelerator. I couldn't stop thinking that something terrible had happened. I needed to pull it together. Wyatt didn't need to see me upset. I took a deep breath, trying to push back the agonizing panic spreading through my chest. I hated it. What if Wyatt had one of his meltdowns when Ms. Daniels left? What if Michael lost his temper and hurt him? Damn. I was so sick of worrying all the time. Sick of being scared.

It was just starting to get dark when I pulled up in Michael's driveway. Looking at Michael's house, I found it hard to believe I once called it home. Michael's parents bought it for us as a wedding present. They wanted us to have the perfect place to start our new lives together, and I fell in love with it the moment I saw it. It didn't take us long to make the place ours, and I actually loved living there. That was a long time ago. Now, it seemed so unfamiliar, haunting. The porch light was on, revealing all the leaves and dirt scattered by the front door. I shook my head as I thought about how hard I used to work to keep the place clean. I knocked on the door and tried to be patient as I waited for someone to answer. The door swung open, and Michael greeted me with an angry snarl on his face.

When he didn't say anything, I said, "Mrs. Daniels called, and I came to see if everything is okay with Wyatt."

"Of course, you did," he growled.

"Look, I don't want to get into an argument with you about this. Just go tell Wyatt I'm here to get him."

He stood in the doorway, arms crossed, with a smug look on his face and said, "Can't do that."

"And why's that?" I asked, trying to hold back my anger. It was so hard for me not to cuss at him. A million profanities were sitting at the tip of my tongue, but I kept them to myself, knowing I needed to keep my cool.

"He's not here," he said with his eyebrow raised in defiance.

"What do you mean he's not here? Ms. Daniels called ten minutes ago and said she left him here with you." He repulsed me. I couldn't believe the man standing in front of me was someone I'd actually cared about; someone I had once loved. Looking at him now made my skin crawl.

"The little shit ran off. Just like always, he can't take it when someone tells him no. If you stopped…" Anger surged through me, and I wanted to strangle him for not giving a shit that our son had disappeared. He should be worried, scared out of his mind, but he hadn't even tried to go and find him.

"Damn it, Michael! Your eight-year-old son ran away, and you didn't even go look for him?" I shouted, turning to head back to my car. "You're unbelievable!" As soon as I got in, I started up the engine and headed to our secret spot, praying that Wyatt was there and that he was okay.

Get the rest of *Stitch*,
Book 2 in the Satan's Fury series, here:
http://tinyurl.com/hzg9nfb.